"What's it going to take for you to trust me, Madison?"

That trust question had simmered unspoken between Madison and Grant from the start. But now that it was in the open, all she wanted to do was shove it back into unspoken silence.

Trust was hard for her, and for just cause. Still, Grant deserved an answer, so she gave him the only one she could. "I don't know."

"Since I hired on with you at Lost, Inc., you've put me through test after test—and you've poured on even more of them in our personal relationship." He lifted a warning finger. "This is *not* the time for you to say we don't have a personal relationship, so don't you dare do it."

She'd like to deny it, but she couldn't. They did have a relationship. It wasn't something either of them needed, but a relationship was there. A mostly adversarial one, but after four months, she had to admit there was also a spark between them that promised they could be very good together...maybe.

Books by Vicki Hinze

Love Inspired Suspense

**Survive the Night*
**Christmas Countdown*
**Torn Loyalties*

*Lost, Inc.

VICKI HINZE

is an award-winning author of nearly thirty novels, four nonfiction books and hundreds of articles published in as many as sixty-three countries. She lives in Florida with her husband, near her children and grands, and she gets cranky if she must miss one of their ball games. Vicki loves to visit with readers and invites you to join her at vickihinze.com or on Facebook.

TORN LOYALTIES

VICKI HINZE

Love Inspired

Recycling programs for this product may not exist in your area.

ISBN-13: 978-0-373-44525-7

TORN LOYALTIES

This edition published by arrangement with Love Inspired Books.

www.LoveInspiredBooks.com

Printed in U.S.A.

I will go before thee, and make the crooked places straight: I will break in pieces the gates of brass, and cut in sunder the bars of iron.

—*Isaiah* 45:2

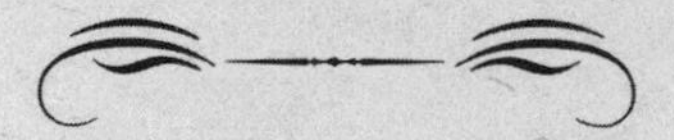

To David, who understands that
to have a friend you must be a friend—and is.
With love and blessings,
Vicki

ONE

Under the cover of deep darkness, Madison McKay slid on her belly in the dirt, lifted the binoculars to her eyes, then peered through a break in the thick woods and studied the distant top secret facility known as the Nest.

It had grown. A lot. In her days as an analyst there, the majority of the structures, a labyrinth of bunkers, had been built underground. Now, not one but four large buildings jutted into the night sky. A wide stretch of asphalt surrounded them, forming a clearing that ensured any approach would be noticed. Armed guards stood posted every twenty feet on the ground near concrete barricades, their backs to the buildings, and more soldiers were staggered on the rooftops. Obviously the commander expected something unusual to happen.

An attack? Unlikely. Only a handful of people assigned to the military installation surrounding the Nest knew the facility hidden at its core existed. So what had the Nest on high alert?

Her stomach burned; her fingers tingled. Northwest

Florida had pretty mild winters, but being out in the woods, exposed to stiff winds and lying flat on the cold ground was enough to numb her gloved fingers and the tip of her masked nose. The stomach burn was acid due to sheer nerves.

Getting caught on the base without authorization would be bad, but getting caught on the perimeter of the Nest…

Not daring to think about the consequences, she cut off those thoughts, and kept watch.

Hours passed. Her eyelids grew heavy, then heavier, lulling her to doze off. She fought the temptation. *Stay awake, Madison. Of all places, here—must stay alert.*

Her resolve redoubled, she kept her breathing shallow, hoping that the mask would keep her exhaled breaths from fogging the air. Even something that slight from this distance could be noted. She kept watching, kept waiting.

Dawn threatened. Soon it would expose her, and in the past four hours, the only noteworthy observations she'd seen were changing of the guards. The soldiers had been relieved and replaced every hour, and that frequency proved telling. Whatever event or threat they expected hadn't yet passed and the commander wanted the soldiers fresh, sharp and on their toes.

In the year she'd been stationed at the Nest, they'd only been on high alert once, for a practice drill in a readiness exercise that had lasted less than two hours. A string of forty-seven eighteen-wheelers had been stopped at the main facility's outer gate. Soldiers had driven the trucks into the Nest, parked at the loading docks and unloaded boxes. The trucks were then returned to the outer gates and their drivers departed with them. The installation had been deemed ready.

Ready for what? No one, not even Madison, who analyzed delivery efficiency of the boxed contents defined only by one-word codes like *Seeds* or *Purifier,* had a clue.

But this alert was different, and two facts proved it: the absence of activity during the alert negated it being a readiness exercise drill, and the tension in the guards proved whatever initiated the alert was not ordinary.

The first signs of dawn pierced the horizon, tingeing it with a thin, pale streak that would soon thicken to daybreak. Her instincts told her to stay put, but she didn't dare. If discovered, she'd never be in a position to expose the truth. The commander would see to that… and possibly to a lot more.

Disappointment battered her. Tonight, after the St. Valentine's ball, she'd try again. Whatever happened here would happen at night.

The wind gusted. Madison's eyes teared. She blinked hard and fast. If the commander and/or his vice commander had done what she suspected, she had to be vigilant and cautious. She was the only thing left standing between them and their possible actions, and those actions could not happen again. Not on her watch. No more lost ones could be sacrificed here. They must find their way home….

Tonight. Tomorrow night. Six months of nights—

whatever it takes, Madison promised herself, then rose to a crouch and scanned the woods. Stealth and hyperalert, noting nothing unexpected, she moved from bush to tree through the thick woods, stepping lightly to avoid creating magnified sounds of dry leaves and twigs crunching underfoot.

With a scant fifteen minutes to spare before daylight exposed her, she left the restricted area and reached the public highway, then sprinted in the woods alongside the road to the sheltered spot where she'd parked her car to hide it from view.

Something odd was definitely going on out there. Whether or not it was connected to her case, she had no idea—yet. Bitterness filled her throat. Swallowing it, she eased into her silver Jaguar still hidden by darkness and shut the door.

"You want to explain what you're doing out there?"

Madison's heart rocketed. A man in her car. *Oh, no.* She'd been caught!

Madison squinted in the half-light, trying to identify the deeply shadowed silhouette of the man in her passenger seat. She recognized him.

Grant Deaver!

Her heart rate shot off the charts, and she inwardly groaned. Given the choice of a firing squad of the guards or this man, she'd take the firing squad. Them, she knew she couldn't trust. But *Grant?* The jury was still out on him. "You want to explain how you got into my car?"

He held up a key. "I used this."

She should have picked up on his cologne as soon as she opened the door. But she'd been so lost in thought that she'd missed it. *Bad mistake.* "Funny, I don't recall giving you a key to my vehicle."

"We've been dating since October, Madison," he reminded her. "Totally plausible you did and forgot it."

She hadn't forgotten a thing. He'd found the spare key she stowed in a magnetic case under the back bumper. "For the record, while you're endearing, your being here is not." He'd scared ten years off her, though she didn't mention it. She'd learned the hard way that exposing vulnerabilities was often interpreted as giving others a license to use them against you. Yes, they were dating. *Keep your friends close and your enemies closer.* But she strongly suspected he was under orders to spy on her and her staff. Of course, she kept him close. How else could she protect her staff or herself? That she found him attractive anyway, well, that was a challenge she just had to fight. "Why are you following me—and where's *your* car?"

"No car."

"You walked all the way out hcrc?" It was ten miles into North Bay proper. Why would he do that? And how had he known where she'd be? Fair questions she needed answered after she got away from this facility. She cranked the engine and pulled over the deep shoulder and onto the road.

"My transportation is insignificant." He frowned at her. "And gauging by what I've observed—you pulling surveillance on an off-limits, highly classified military installation—you're hardly in a position to ask anyone questions." He lifted an irritated hand. "Dressed in covert operation gear with greasepaint smeared all over your face." She passed him her binoculars. "What are you doing out there at all, much less dressed like that? Are you trying to get yourself shot?"

She lowered the mask, let its strings loosely loop her neck and braked to a stop at the traffic light. *The office or home?*

Definitely not home. Not with him in the car. She'd shower and change at the office. It'd be hours before anyone else arrived. She hung a left and cruised past the sign to North Bay. "Since this is my car and you're in it uninvited, I'm perfectly positioned to ask whatever questions I want." She spared him a glance. "Why are you following me and how did you find me?"

Concern and anger feuded in his eyes, shone in the reflective light from the dash. "You were edgy all day—even more so than usual, which is saying something. You denied anything was up, so I had a friend drop me off."

So now two people had followed her and knew where she'd gone. *Oh, definitely not good.* "So because I chose not to answer you, you have the right to shadow me?" She slid him a mild frown. "If I wanted to disclose, I'd disclose." Inside, a part of her felt pleased he was concerned and wanted to protect her. Not surprising; he was a Christian, but one in an awkward position. She buried her emotional pleasure under the real facts. No way did she dare trust him. "Who brought you out here?"

"Mrs. Renault."

Her assistant. Pins of betrayal pricked and peppered her skin. "You're kidding me."

"She knows the danger, Madison."

She did. She'd been married to the former base commander. Still, telling Grant where Madison was and bringing him out there? What had Mrs. Renault been thinking?

"Don't get knotted up at her. I was worried about you and so was she." He paused and lowered his voice, not bothering to remove the sarcasm lacing it. "Worry. That's something normal people do when they care about someone—in between the times they're questioning their sanity for caring for someone as stubborn as you."

She opened her mouth to object. Before she got out the first word, he cut her off.

"You know what? Don't even bother. This has gone on long enough." He sighed irritably and dragged a hand through his short brown hair. "What's it going to take for you to trust me, Madison?"

That trust question had simmered unspoken between them from the start. She'd wished a hundred times in the past four months she could just drag the matter out into the open. But now that it *was* in the open, all she wanted to do was shove it back into the shadows.

Instead, she clicked her blinker with her pinkie, signaling a left turn. Trust was hard for her, maybe impossible, and for just cause. *Once betrayed, twice shy.* Still, he deserved an answer, so she gave him the only one she could. "I don't know."

"Since I hired on with you at Lost, Inc., you've put me through test after test—and you've poured on even more of them in our personal relationship." He lifted a warning finger. "This is *not* the time for you to say we don't have a personal relationship."

She'd like to deny it, but she couldn't. First, it wasn't true. They did have a relationship. A mostly adversarial one, but after four months under horrific conditions, she had to admit there was also a spark between them that promised they could be very good together… maybe. Eventually. And, keeping it real and fair, she had tested him to the max professionally and personally. Every single time, he'd passed with flying colors. Yet even that hadn't removed her doubts and resolved her trust issues.

"Not disputing the relationship," he said. "That's progress. Yet you don't know what it's going to take to trust me. And if you don't know, then obviously I can't know." He sighed again. More deeply. "So let's try a different question. How about keeping it simple—just tell me about this jaunt of yours tonight?"

Boldly stated, and a fair question. Right after the agency's open house during the annual Fall Festival back in October, she'd been *invited* to the military installation and quizzed about a security breach at the Nest. It had been easy to see they were after someone to blame. She'd countered by hiring Grant. He'd just left active duty working in the Office of Special Investigations for the very commander and vice commander who had questioned her, and she needed to keep an eye on him. *Keep your friends close and your enemies closer.* Commander Talbot and Vice Commander Dayton were also the reason she was watching the Nest. She strongly suspected those two men had links to two civilian murders that unfortunately everyone *except her* deemed solved. The cases had been officially closed.

That was her initial connection to Grant Deaver. And while he hadn't sold her out—yet—he had reported Lost, Inc., events back to Talbot and Dayton, purportedly defending her agency. Still, the commander had a security breach at the Nest, and he and his vice commander were trying their best to blame it on someone at her agency. With Grant reporting to them, how *could* she trust him?

Tempted to blast that question at him, she fingered the Purple Heart medal in her jacket pocket to steady herself. This would be a dangerous time to lose her temper. Trust him with the truth? Oh, how she wished she could. "I can't answer that, either."

He grumbled under his breath. "How can you be attracted enough to me to date me but not trust me at all? I don't get it, Madison."

"Neither do I," she admitted, hating being put on the spot like this. "Ordinarily, I wouldn't be attracted and I'd never put you on my payroll—"

"I think I've just been insulted."

Two hundred pounds and six feet of bruised male ego

she did not need. "That came out wrong." She glanced at him then back at the road. "Of course I'm attracted to you. What woman wouldn't be? What I meant was there's something about you that gets to me, but I wish it didn't."

"Because I'm on your payroll."

"Not really." Oh, she didn't want to get into this. Weary already, she didn't want to resurrect old wounds.

He flicked at the door handle with his fingertips. "You know, I'd really like to get out of this car, walk away from you and never look back—"

Panic threatened. "Grant, don't. Please." She didn't want him to go. She wanted… She didn't know what she wanted, but she wanted him with her.

"I won't." His frown deepened to a scowl. "Because as unfair as this situation is, I understand, and I'm as conflicted about you as you are about me."

The attraction was mutual…and mutually disdainful. That pricked more than her pride. It pricked her heart. "Sometimes God has a bizarre sense of humor."

"Apparently." He lifted a finger. "Watch that deer."

Spotting it on the edge of the road, Madison slowed and veered into the other lane to give the animal a wide berth. "Listen, I admit that this case has me worked up, and I'm touchier than usual because of it. It's also been a really long night. Can we talk about this later?" After she thawed out would be good.

"'This case,' you said. So you were at the Nest because of the David Pace and Beth Crane murders." Grant's frustration showed in his expression.

David Pace and Beth Crane were both reporters who'd been murdered after asking questions about the Nest. No one outside a very small group even knew the Nest existed. Pace and Crane were not in that loop. That much both she and Grant knew. She didn't confirm or deny Grant's suspicion.

"Madison, those murders were solved. Gary Crawford confessed to killing them both. What more do you need to let go of this obsession that Talbot and Dayton are responsible for their deaths?"

She pulled into the office parking lot, then turned in her seat to look into the face of the man she cared more for than any man in her life and trusted less than any man she'd ever let get within shouting distance. "I need the truth. I believe David and Beth were sacrificed. I've been sacrificed, and I won't stand by and let it happen to them, too."

Grant's expression softened. "They're not lost, Madison. They're dead."

Her heart clenched. "The truth about what happened to them and why it happened is lost. That's just as bad. Their families deserve to know the facts."

His mouth flattened to a slash and he stared out the windshield.

"Grant, you have to understand." Her mouth went ash dry. Weary or not, she forced herself to open old wounds anyway. "When I was on active duty in Afghanistan, I was on a mission that went south. Because of my job, my superiors sacrificed me. You know I was taken prisoner, but there are things you don't know."

He knew she'd worked in the intelligence realm, and asked, "Like what?"

She worked hard to keep the anger still simmering inside her out of her voice. "They knew I was alive but classified me killed in action, anyway—to avoid an international incident, I was later told." She cocked her head. "We can't admit we have spies out there, you know."

"That's standard operating procedure."

"Except when it happens to you." The back of her nose burned. "I gave everything and I was disposable. Just one of many, and leaving me behind was expedient—"

"You were treated no differently than anyone else. Everyone in Intel knows that's the way it works."

"Exactly. Operatives and agents know, but my parents didn't sign on to that. They're not in Intel and they didn't know. My family should have been told the truth—I believed they would be told the truth—but they weren't. They were told I was dead." A hard lump lodged in her throat. Her eyes stung. "For the next eighteen months, I was a POW and they mourned my death."

"Eighteen months. I knew you'd gotten a Purple Heart, but I had no idea you were held that long." Grant stilled. Stared at her. "How did they finally get you out?"

Her heart twisted. "Did you not hear me? They did nothing but forget me and leave me to rot in a four-by-six cell." She hiked her chin. "*I* got *myself* out. I watched, waited and learned. They had me working in the kitchen, which included going to market. I studied everything, watched everyone, looking for weaknesses and information I could use. There was one guard who was particularly slow on the uptake. He'd escort me to the market now and then. One day when he did, I spotted an opening, and I took it. I escaped."

"Totally on your own?"

"Totally." The bitterness at that surged in her. Mingled with the anger, it proved too strong to fight. "It took me four months to make my way back to the States.

"No one would officially help me, Grant. I didn't exist."

"So you had no money, no papers, and yet you managed to get back home?"

"Money can be earned and papers bought." It hadn't been easy. Parts of the ordeal had been horrifically dangerous and difficult. Getting out of Pakistan had been a nightmare, and the ship… She shuddered just thinking of the ship. Old and moldy—she was posing as a young man and working as a deckhand—it had been awful. And yet she had prayed through it and made it. "I prepositioned funds and papers but it took time and finesse to get to them. Yet that's not the point. The point is that for all the time I was held captive and trying to get home—until the moment I knocked on my parents' front door and my mother answered, my parents thought I was dead."

Never would Madison forget the ravages of grief in them, their utter shock at seeing her, or their overwhelming relief of her still being alive and coming home to them.

"I can imagine their relief." He frowned. "You're cold." Reaching over, he adjusted the heater to take out the chill. "So what happened when you showed up at headquarters?"

"They gave me a Purple Heart and offered me a promotion with a stateside slot."

"You kept the medal but departed the fix."

She nodded. "No way was I staying active duty after they abandoned me. But the medal was different."

"You'd earned it."

It'd taken months for her physical wounds to heal. But the emotional ones cut even deeper and some remained raw. "I did earn it, but no." She let him see the steel in her gaze. "I still believe in the spirit it embodies. I trust that spirit and the medal reminds me that there are others out there like me."

"That's why you opened Lost, Inc. To bring the lost home."

She nodded. Now maybe he'd understand why she couldn't just drop the Pace and Crane murders.

"I'm sorry you went through that." Grant clasped her hand.

"Me, too." She gave him a bittersweet smile. It was a time of trials but also a time that solidified her faith. She'd done the impossible then, and no one knew better than she that she couldn't have done it alone, though she was still working at not being bitter that God hadn't spared her from the trial.

"I understand why you want the truth on the murders, Madison, but I believe you already have it. What I still don't understand is you going out to the Nest." Grant squeezed her hand. "I mean, what can you learn by staring at the outside of the facility that will prove anything?"

Madison stiffened, and bit her tongue. *Speak it in anger, regret it in calm.* She'd eaten enough words in her war of wits and wills with him already. "If I knew the answer to that, I wouldn't have to go out there, would I?" She left the car.

The slammed car door signaled Grant to follow her.

She opened the office door, turned off the alarm, flipped on the lights and headed upstairs to the kitchen. Hot coffee would be good.

"I'll do that." He took the coffeepot out of her hands. "You go get cleaned up before anyone else gets here. Out there all night, you're probably half-frozen. A hot shower will thaw you out."

Why did he do that? Just when she wanted to bark his head off, he turned around and did something thoughtful and caring. "Thank you." She walked to the door, then paused and looked back at him, shrugging out of his coat.

Tall and broad shouldered, he was in great shape and obviously had kept up his physical training regimen. Her stomach clutched. Looking at him did crazy things to her. It always had. From the very first time she'd laid eyes on him, without a word or an ounce of effort, he'd begun chipping away at the protective barriers she'd studiously built around her heart. She resented that but seemed helpless to stop it. Still, she was determined. Caring about a man she couldn't trust was absurdly foolish, and she was not a foolish woman.

She shoved back the black hoodie covering her hair. Long silver-blond strands fell loose down her back. "Are you ever going to tell me why you really followed me?"

"I did tell you."

"No, you gave me a line about me being edgy and you being worried."

His square jaw tightened. "It wasn't a line." He draped his coat on the brass tree, poured water into the coffeemaker, flipped the switch and then turned to answer her. "I followed you because I don't want you to end up dead."

What *exactly* did he mean? He'd followed her to the Nest, but he hadn't interceded. He'd waited in her car. So where did he sense danger to her? His expression had never been more sober or serious, or more closed, giving nothing away. "You agree with me, then? You think Commander Talbot and Vice Commander Dayton are involved in a cover-up, too?"

Grant frowned and hedged. "I think if you get caught spying on the Nest, you're going to get shot."

Madison frowned back at him. "How can you ignore Talbot and Dayton when you know they're trying their best to blame someone at my agency for the security breach?"

David Pace and Beth Crane had been reporters for

WKME, a local TV station. Separately, three years apart, they'd gone to Talbot to confirm tips from sources they'd been given about the Nest. The facility buried in the woods in the center of a military installation so highly classified that even those assigned to the base didn't know the Nest was there—*that* Nest. Talbot had denied David Pace's and Beth Crane's tips and in short order, both had been murdered. But their tips had been accurate. And that meant someone definitely had breached security.

"I'm not ignoring anything or anyone."

But he was. Commander Talbot was up for a congressional appointment. Vice Commander Dayton was up for Talbot's job. A security breach by someone under their command could ax those promotions. In short, Talbot and/or Dayton needed a scapegoat and they intended to find one at Lost, Inc.

"They have to look at everyone in your agency, Madison, and you know it."

Lost, Inc., was a logical, rich target. Everyone working for her was former military and had served at least one assignment at the Nest. None of them would breach security, but as they were no longer under Talbot's or Dayton's command, any one of them would serve the purpose of taking the fall and keeping the commanders' promotions safe.

Serial killer Gary Crawford had supposedly killed David Pace. Beth Crane had been deemed the victim of a home invasion until Crawford's apprehension, when he'd confessed to killing them both. But Madison wasn't buying it. Serial killers confessed to everything to embellish their legacy and incite fear in others. Beth Crane and, three years later, David Pace had exposed the security breach by asking Talbot for confirmation of the Nest's existence, and Madison was sure that's how they'd ended up dead. "You know no one here would—"

Grant leaned back against the counter, and crossed his arms. "What I know is that if you get caught out there spying, you'll lose more than your career."

The finality in Grant's tone signaled he was finished talking about this, and so was she. How could she convince him with no more proof than her instincts? Her challenge was that simple.

And that complex.

Madison showered, then dressed in black slacks, a teal sweater and flats. She left her hair down, applied lotion to her wind-chafed skin and then returned to the kitchen.

Grant sat at the table drinking a cup of coffee from a camouflage-print mug. He cast her a weary, pensive look but said nothing.

Her favorite Minnie Mouse mug sat on the counter beside the coffeepot—he noticed and remembered everything about her, even her preferred coffee mug—and she filled it, then joined him at the table. Did he remember details about her because of professional or personal reasons? His profiling training or a genuine affection for her? Unsure, she sipped, then said, "You're pretty steamed at me, aren't you?"

He shook his head. "I'm worried. I want you to promise me you'll stay away from the Nest."

"I can't do that." She wouldn't even stay away if she trusted him with all her heart. "I've made my reasons clear. I'm stalled on my case until I find new information or until Talbot releases the satellite images under the Freedom of Information Act." Hopefully, he'd do that before she died of old age. She'd requested them two months ago, during the Christmas cruise she and Grant had taken with a group of friends.

Grant knew as well as she did that those images of David Pace's exploded car would prove whether or not it had been placed where it had been found before or after the explosion, which would prove whether or not David Pace had been in it when it had blown up. His medical file was sealed. *Why?* Right after Gary Crawford's arrest and confessions, she'd received a tip that Pace's body hadn't been burned. *Why that tip? Why to her?* People didn't take those kinds of reporting risks without reason.

Grant lifted a hand. "The man died from natural causes. An embolism. You saw the coroner's report."

"So did you. It was a lie. It had to be a lie, or the embolism had to be induced." Grant couldn't be buying into that report. "There were no signs of anything like that in his medical history—nothing that points to there being any problem. He was young and healthy." And Grant knew as well as she that inducing an embolism was a military tactic. Carrying out a kill order? Emergency termination? She shuddered.

"For pity's sake." Grant lifted his cup. "You talked to the coroner."

"No, I didn't," she disputed him. "I *tried* to talk to him, but the coroner refused to take my call or to meet with me. His assistant referred me to the public report, informed me that the case was sealed, and then she totally shut down. Why would the case be sealed unless he's hiding something?"

"Oh, gee, I don't know. Maybe because Crawford was a serial killer working for Homeland Security and that knowledge would undermine public trust in the entire agency? Remember, Homeland Security sealed the file, not the local authorities, and Crawford hasn't yet been tried for his other victims' murders. Or maybe the coroner just didn't want to waste his time on a closed case when he has a ton of open ones to work on." Grant dropped his voice. "Or it could be that the coroner has known you all your life and he's trying to keep you from putting yourself in the crosshairs of people who will hurt you."

"That sounds as if you think there might be some validity to my theory."

"I'm trying to be fair. The case is closed. Crawford did confess to both murders. The coroner did sign off on the Pace report. But if on the outside chance you're right about this—and I don't believe you are—then for this conspiracy and cover-up to work, the coroner would have had to sign off on a false report, and I don't think he would."

"Under normal circumstances, I'd say no." She'd

known the man her whole life. He'd given her and her best friend, Maggie Mason, pony rides at the annual town festivals when they were children, and when they'd tried smoking cigarettes as teens and had gotten sick and gone to the morgue to save him a trip to pick up their bodies, he'd assured them they weren't dying—but if he caught them smoking again, they'd wish they were. "Yet these circumstances are not normal. With Homeland Security involved… They, or the commander, could have pressured him."

"Through Homeland Security, the commander might have exerted influence," Grant conceded. "But it's highly unlikely."

Grant defending his former commander wasn't surprising. She well recalled her own defensive posture right up until the moment she realized she'd been abandoned. "It's not impossible."

"No, it's not impossible." Grant sipped from his mug, then set it on the table and reached for her hand.

She laid it atop his and he curled his fingers, pressing their heated palms. "Madison, what if you're right? Say Talbot or Dayton were involved in the murders and cover-ups. Say they did exert influence and the coroner did forge the report. Would people with the power and authority to do those things hesitate to kill again?" Grant gently squeezed her fingertips. "Don't you see that by pushing this, you're putting yourself in danger?"

His hand trembled. She loved that, and wished she didn't. "I know—"

"Have you forgotten that just for investigating a classified project to which you once had authorized access, you can be declared a security threat—and the charges will stick? They can declare you a domestic terrorist and detain you indcfinitely."

"That's absurd." She grunted. "They can't—"

His expression turned flat. "Check recent legislation. They can and will." He clasped her arms. "Forget this, Madison. Please. You know the lengths they've gone to since inception to keep the Nest off everyone's radar. If the security breach and your two murders are connected…" He swallowed hard, clearly conflicted. "Do you think for a second they wouldn't stop you from exposing them by any means necessary?" He rubbed at his neck. "Good grief, the entire government's behind them."

Whether or not the people in most of those positions knew it, the government *was* behind them. And the measures taken to hide the project had been extraordinary. The need-to-know loop on the Nest was extremely tight. "I know all this, okay?" He cared. He might have to spy on her, but he also cared. It showed clearly whenever he got emotional, and right now Grant Deaver was extremely emotional. She softened her voice. "The bottom line is I believe they've buried the truth on two civilian murders. I believe it, Grant. And if they did and I do nothing, and the need arises, they'll murder again. How many have to be lost before—"

"For the tenth time, the victims in this case are not lost, they're dead."

"The truth about them *is* lost," she repeated, stroking his arm.

His mouth flattened. "Nothing you discover will bring them back. Their family members have buried them, mourned, and they're healing, Madison. Think of Ian," he said, speaking of Beth Crane's husband, who worked for Madison at the agency. "Don't rip open the wounds when all it's going to do is put him back to square one mourning all over again."

Grant was right, of course. It was for that very reason she hadn't said one word to Ian about her investigation. She didn't want to hurt anyone, especially Ian when he was finally healing, but letting the truth be obscured was fundamentally wrong. Even Ian would never settle for letting someone—*anyone*—get away with murder.

Grant lowered his gaze from the ceiling and his voice dropped to a hush. "Look, I know how important finding the lost ones is to you. Even when everyone else gives up, you never do. I admire that about you. But this with the Nest… You're in trouble with this—if you get caught, the kind of trouble that'll make your POW days seem like a walk in the park."

"I'm aware of the risks. But my safety isn't my main concern." She looked him right in the eye, let him see the truth. "I'm right about this. I know it. Can you just trust me?"

"I do trust you. My trust in you has never been an issue."

He was right. The issue was her trusting him, and now he stood genuinely worried. She hated that. "I realize you disagree with me on all of this. You have doubts. But I don't, and if they get away with killing two people, what's to stop them from killing four, or forty-four?" She set down her mug. "No. No, I can't worry about the risks. I have to do the right thing."

"Hardheaded, stubborn—" His voice faded into a grumble.

She pretended to be deaf as a stone. Deeply worried and afraid for her, he needed to vent, and she needed a minute to get her insides to stop shaking. Busying herself, she refocused, refilling her mug at the coffeepot, then returned to the table. "The bottom line is that if Talbot or Dayton are behind the murders, they won't risk their futures on Crawford getting a whim and withdrawing his confessions. He could recant at any time. They're going to silence him because neither of them can afford not to—personally or as Nest commanders."

"Even if Crawford recanted, no one would believe him."

"No, but in the commanders' elevated positions—their promotions will come quickly now, right?" When Grant nodded, Madison finished. "They won't risk a blemish on their records, and they know that politically a Crawford confession would become a public issue under microscopic scrutiny in the media."

"That much is true."

"They'll prevent that." If she were right, Crawford's days were numbered. "There's another nugget that is even more compelling."

"What?"

Madison leaned forward and dropped her voice. "If Crawford recants, the uproar about David Pace and Beth Crane will pass. But another uproar won't, and it'll have heads rolling at the highest levels."

The color leaked from Grant's face. "No. No way. Neither Talbot nor Dayton will go public. They wouldn't jeopardize national security for media ratings or political points. That is what you're saying, right?"

"Under the right conditions, they would."

"What right conditions? It'd be political suicide."

"Not if they leaked every single crumb on the Nest under the protection of a congressional hearing. They'd claim they had no choice but to disclose, Congress would back them on that, and the focus would definitely shift away from them, Crawford and the murders and land squarely on the Nest."

Grant's hand on his mug shook, and his eyes narrowed. "The need-to-know loop would never allow that testimony to take place."

"Which is why I think they'll get rid of Crawford before he can recant his confessions." She rubbed at a dull throb in her temple. "Once he does, then neither Talbot and Dayton nor anyone else in the loop can stonewall Congress indefinitely. For a while, yes, but then something will give. It always does."

Grant paused a moment, clearly thinking. "We know from working there that the need-to-know loop will keep word of the Nest sequestered by any necessary means."

Madison agreed. "Yes." Like the others, she'd had restricted access to the Nest, allowed only in her specific area. She was as clueless as everyone else about what was at the Nest and why the facility existed at all, but the secrecy of the facility was made clear to everyone who knew about it. "These deductions have left me with another question. I can't answer it, but maybe you can."

He smoothed a thumb over her shirtsleeve at her wrist, his expression guarded. "What question?"

"Why?" Madison looked him right in the eye. "What is so important about that facility that they could be killing people to keep it a secret?"

TWO

Mrs. Renault appeared at Madison's office door. "You're back."

Madison nodded, biting her tongue about Mrs. Renault dropping Grant off out at the Nest last night. "Is it time for the morning report?"

Tall and lithe, the fiftyish Mrs. Renault entered, wearing a slim skirt and fitted top. Her taupe heels clicked softly on the hardwood floor. "I thought with the Valentine's ball tonight at the club, you'd be home resting."

"No, I've been having a heated discussion with Grant."

"And you're not happy with me for taking him out there."

"Actually, no, I'm not."

"Fine." She pulled out her pad and poised her pen.

"That's all the explanation I get?" Madison fingered her Purple Heart, rolled it over in her palm.

"You were in danger. You needed backup."

Madison resisted the urge to raise her voice. "I don't trust him."

"You have trust issues with everyone but me," Mrs. Renault said, decidedly calm.

"After last night, I think I should be on the fence about you, too."

If that comment ruffled her, Mrs. Renault didn't show it. "Well, I trust Grant."

Madison envied her that. She was coming to care for this man. She yearned to trust him. But she just didn't dare. Still, curiosity got the better of her. "Why?" Mrs. Renault's instincts were usually flawless, but the woman knew he'd been reporting agency activities to Talbot and Dayton.

"If Grant had reported anything negative on us, we'd all have been hauled in for questioning. We haven't been. My guess is Grant has done nothing more than tell the commander we've been working internally to assure no one here breached security by telling the reporters anything about the Nest. He's probably been instrumental in keeping heat off the entire agency."

Madison hadn't considered that possibility.

"You must remember, Madison, Grant is in a delicate position. He's subject to recall for two years after the date he officially came off active duty. He can't refuse to report, though I imagine feeling about you as he does, he wishes he could."

Didn't she wish she knew how he felt about her? Wouldn't it be a gift to be sure? "I know he can't refuse them." She'd gone through that two-year period herself.

"So he's done his duty. No more and no less."

"And I shouldn't fault him for it."

"He took an oath, as did you." Mrs. Renault looked over, and gave her the infamous Renault lift of the brow. "Would you respect a man who made an oath and didn't keep it?"

"No." She wouldn't, but didn't have to like admitting it. Grant's position wasn't lost on her. He was a man torn between the dictates of his faith and his country. And if her wishes and Mrs. Renault's instincts were right, he was also torn between faith, country and her: a woman he cared about. Being pulled in three different directions had to keep him up nights, but she was up nights, too. She cared about him, but should she? Was caring about him putting her and her staff in jeopardy? If he was being honest with her, then no. But was he? Considering the pressure on him from all sides… she wasn't sure. Odds were, he wasn't sure himself. "Grant reporting shouldn't be necessary. Talbot and Dayton know what we do here. You'd think they'd see merit in it." Madison sipped from her mug, stared at the sun streaking in through the white sheers covering the window. "In four years, we've gone from zero to success by any standards. That should be enough."

"You're assuming they don't see merit in our work, and you know anecdotal evidence can't be enough to negate a hard look when anything classified is involved. The Nest is a lot more…sensitive."

She did know, but she didn't have to like that, either. She looked at the Purple Heart medal and spoke from her heart. "The problem is, I want to trust him."

"You've developed strong feelings for him?"

"I wouldn't go that far."

"Of course you wouldn't. How far would you go?"

"I hate it when you do that." Madison frowned. Since her days as a POW, she was cautious with her trust. Betrayed and burned as she'd been—who wouldn't be? "Why do you make me admit what I feel, especially when I don't want to feel anything?" Madison let her see her exasperation. "I don't want to care about him. I don't want to trust him."

"But you just said you do want to trust him…."

"See what I mean? He stirs things inside me and makes me so crazy I don't even know my own mind."

"At the risk of rattling you even more—your hands are shaking—I believe you're making yourself crazy. He's just being Grant, doing the best he can in an awkward situation."

Madison groaned and kept staring at the medal. It meant so much to her, and Grant now knew it. Though she'd been sacrificed and the bond had been broken with her superiors, the bond between her and the spirit of the medal, her nation, her relationship with her family and her faith, remained intact. Grant not only had understood but also had said he felt the same way, though when faith and duty to country conflicted, it caused a lot of internal challenges. That he'd shared that revelation made another chink in the armor around her heart. "He seems honorable—as if he's trying so hard to do the right thing all around. I know it can't be easy, yet..." She sighed. "I feel like a horrible person for having doubts and as if anyone with sense should have doubts... This wouldn't be nearly so hard if I didn't... but I do." She let Mrs. Renault see the misery in her eyes. "I...care about him."

Sympathy reflected in Mrs. Renault's eyes. "I can see that you do."

In a cold sweat, Madison met Mrs. Renault's gaze. "I think he genuinely cares about me, too." It cost her a lot to admit that out loud.

"Uh-huh." Mrs. Renault put her pen down atop her pad on a little table beside her chair. "Madison, are you falling in love with Grant?"

"Oh, I hope not." She nearly wilted and a lump formed in her throat.

"Why? Do you know?"

"I'm afraid I do." Trusting her heart had gotten her captured and taken prisoner, had changed the entire course of her life. "My heart can't be trusted." Madison walked over to the wall and pressed a button on the back of a landscape painting of the cove done by her friend Maggie Mason. It was the view from the club's gazebo, less than a half mile from Madison's office, and one of Madison's favorite places on earth. A section of wall slid open. Madison gently placed the medal inside.

When she turned, Mrs. Renault stood waiting. "I hate to say it, but trusted or not, I'm afraid your heart will settle long before your mind."

"Wits and wisdom, not your heart, get you through hard times."

"Perhaps it's all of them—your heart *and* wits and wisdom." Mrs. Renault returned to her seat. "That's what happened when I fell in love with John." She harrumphed softly, in the refined way only she could. "Oh, how my mind rebelled against loving that man."

"Why?" Madison couldn't believe it. She always seemed so sure-footed on everything.

"I was a military brat, and I vowed never to fall in love with a military man. I wanted roots."

"But you married John anyway."

"Yes, I did. And given the chance, I would again."

She had been happy with him, not that anyone doubted it for a second. Such a shame he died so young. "So your heart won the battle. That's what you're telling me, isn't it?"

"Wits and wisdom have their value but the heart always wins the battle. That's what I'm telling you."

That was not what she'd hoped to hear. "Maybe so, but I'm not giving up yet."

Madison shut the vault, returned to her desk then sat down and stared at the fireplace filled not with wood but with strings of twinkling little lights. She said, "I don't understand him. He listens but he doesn't hear me."

"That's been the problem with men and relationships since there have been men and relationships." Mrs. Renault cocked her head. "I take it that you've discussed this communication challenge with him?"

Madison expelled a hard breath. "I have. The problem is, this morning when he told me he couldn't walk away from me, either, I was relieved. I was so afraid he would, I was almost sick inside."

"Maybe it was being out in the cold all night."

"No, it was him." Madison fisted her hand. "The only other time I've been that scared is when I was captured."

"Oh, my. Strong emotions."

"Very strong emotions." Madison slid her assistant a wistful look. "I keep praying they'll fizzle and go away."

"Because...?"

"I just told you. I don't trust him."

"But you want to," Mrs. Renault reminded her, her eyes darting a long moment. "I have an idea. Why not give him a real chance? Take a leap of faith? That could ease some pressure on you and be telling."

There was wisdom in the older woman's suggestion. It would allow her to trust him—and with a safety net. The battle in her would cease...maybe. It would definitely ease up. That could make trying it worth a shot. She'd taken a small step, sharing her suspicions about what could come of Crawford and Talbot and Dayton's desire to shift focus. She hadn't even shared that with Mrs. Renault, who had a soft spot for the commander. For that reason alone, Madison prayed the man was innocent of killing Pace and Beth Crane.

"You're going to the St. Valentine's ball together tonight, right?"

Madison nodded.

"Well, one question to answer before you decide. Is your hesitation because you don't trust him on the security breach, or because you don't trust him with your heart?"

Madison didn't dare answer—not even to herself.

Mrs. Renault clearly didn't expect her to. She continued, "Either way, it's a step forward. And it's time you took one."

Madison hadn't dared to trust a man since escaping from Afghanistan. She'd wanted to, tried to, but she just couldn't do it. At times she wondered if she'd ever trust a man again. Since one she'd put her trust in had been responsible for her capture, she couldn't fault herself for that, though her pastor insisted that God wouldn't approve of deeming all men responsible for the sins of one. She wasn't trying to do that. It wasn't them but her own judgment she doubted. Her pastor insisting she was not trusting God shocked her. Was he right?

Unsure, Madison looked at Mrs. Renault. She was right about one thing. If Madison didn't try to step forward, change wouldn't be possible. And maybe her pastor was right, too. Maybe she did need to trust God to put a worthy man in her path.

Grant's image filled Madison's mind—the promise of what could be. Foolish or wise, she didn't know, but this proposal was for one night. She could leap that far, to trust and give him a real chance.

"All right," she told Mrs. Renault. "I'll try."

What could it hurt?

Me. Madison swallowed hard. *God, help me. I'm leaping. Please don't let me regret it.*

A brash young lieutenant with a red nose, bruised knuckles and a name tag that read *Blake* escorted Grant into the commander's windowless inner sanctum.

Commander Talbot sat behind his gleaming desk. Vice Commander Dayton perched on the left of two deep blue leather visitor's chairs. Grant saluted.

"Major Deaver." Talbot returned the salute. "Come in."

Not invited to sit, Grant stood at ease before the desk. "You wanted to see me, sir?"

"Yes." The commander leaned back in his chair, his thinning pate catching the light from the overhead. "How are things going at Lost, Inc.?"

"They're tense, sir." Dayton hadn't said a word. He looked almost bored, though Grant had been in Intel too long to be fooled by that facade. The man wasn't missing a thing. Dressed in combat gear instead of his blues—why? Everyone Grant had come across, from the gate guards to headquarters' security, had been dressed in blues or their regular uniforms today.

"Tense?" The commander stopped rocking his chair.

"Yes, sir." Grant debated over his approach, and decided Talbot had always been reasonable, so he'd just talk straight. "Madison McKay still doesn't trust me."

Dayton guffawed. "Lost your touch with the ladies, eh?"

Caustic, but Grant didn't take it personally. Dayton

had made it an art form. "She's a former operative," Grant said. "She knows the tactics. You either come at her from a genuine place, or you don't get near her at all."

Talbot rubbed at his jaw. "Madison has always had good instincts. They made her an excellent analyst and operative."

"Working with Renée Renault has sharpened them," Dayton said. "You can bank on that."

"Renée is gifted." Talbot drummed his fingers on his desktop and sighed. "Sorry we lost Madison. I hoped she'd change her mind and rejoin us after being home for a while."

Grant had never heard such respect in Dayton's tone as when he'd spoken of Mrs. Renault, and never had anyone other than Commander Talbot called her by her first name. No doubt her military family missed her. But the remark about Madison irked Grant. If they hadn't sacrificed her, maybe they wouldn't have lost her, but the bottom line was Grant didn't want to repeat the mistake and lose her, and the longer this deception went on, the greater the odds were that he would.

Determined to try to do something about that, he shifted the conversation to a place he was more than eager to go. "Crawford accepted responsibility for the security breach. The case is closed." No reaction, so he went on. "How much longer do I have to stay at Lost, Inc., and—?"

Talbot frowned. "Indefinitely."

Grant's heart sank. His stomach knotted. "May I ask why, sir?"

Dayton piped up. "If the commander wanted you to know, he'd tell you. You have your orders, Major."

Grant clamped his jaw. "Yes, sir."

"Ease up, Jeremy," Talbot told Dayton, then swerved his gaze to Grant. "You're absolutely convinced that no one at Lost, Inc., has in any way been involved in the Nest security breach?"

"I am, sir." Silently he prayed no questions came that required him to disclose Madison's jaunt into the Nest's perimeter woods last night.

Dayton, lean and compact with thick muscles, stood up. "Need I remind you that every single individual in that agency is, shall we say, disenchanted with the military?"

"No, sir. I haven't forgotten," Grant said. "They are disenchanted—for just cause."

"In your opinion." Talbot's eyes narrowed. "Doesn't that send up a red flag in your mind that any of them could have breached security, and leaked word of the Nest to the media? Or maybe even to Crawford?"

"Yes, sir. But after a thorough investigation, in my opinion, none did. There's no connection between any of them and Crawford, or to the Nest, beyond their assignments to it during their active-duty days. Crawford, working for Homeland Security, had direct access. He didn't require a leak to know about the Nest. He was briefed on it regularly and personally visited the facility a dozen times."

Worry creased the commander's skin between his eyebrows. "What if I told you that Crawford's access was even more restricted than your own?"

"That changes nothing, sir. He's proven resourceful in the killings we've verified he's done. I've no doubt he could be equally resourceful in gaining access to restricted areas, particularly from the inside." Grant didn't want a long conversation diversion into Gary Crawford. He'd claimed responsibility for the security breach and for the murders. That was that. "I'm convinced that Madison and her staff are innocent, sir."

"Including Renée Renault?"

Grant nodded at the commander.

His eyes narrowed, curious not accusing. "Why?" Talbot was a widower, and he'd been in love with Mrs. Renault since her husband had died. As far as anyone knew, though, it was one-sided and unspoken. Still, Talbot knew her nature well. This was more Talbot testing Grant's judgment. "Actually, Mrs. Renault weighs heavily in my assessment. She would never work for anyone who would cross this country. And Madison is just like Mrs. Renault about that." Grant cleared his throat. "They're patriots, sir. If either of them felt someone at the agency had jeopardized national security, they'd be the first to knock on your door."

That clearly pleased the commander.

It didn't impress Dayton. He stepped closer and stared up into Grant's face. "You realize you're staking your life on that assessment, Major."

Grant lowered his eyes to look at the man. At about

five-nine, Dayton had to tilt back his head to meet Grant's gaze. "Yes, sir."

"That's enough for me." The commander signaled Grant could depart.

"So I can consider the assignment closed?"

"No." The commander glanced at Dayton, then back at Grant. "I think it's best if you stay put for now."

Disappointment hit Grant hard. He was going to lose Madison before he could even win her over. Probably just as well. With secrets and lies between them that he couldn't disclose and resolve, well, losing her now was probably easier on his heart than losing her later. But, man, he wished he didn't have to lose her at all. "Yes, sir." Grant saluted.

"Dismissed," the commander said, then as Grant reached the door, he added, "Major, I'm sure your investigation is thorough, but do keep your eyes and ears open anyway." He laced his hands atop his desk. "I am aware of the awkwardness of your current position, but it is necessary."

Was it? At first, maybe. But now that he'd reported his findings? Grant didn't see the rationale. Not one valid reason he had to remain at the agency, spying on Madison or her entire staff. But there was something in Talbot's eyes. Something Grant couldn't decipher or quite grasp…yet. "Yes, sir."

Grant took the stairs, too irritated to wait for the elevator. Downstairs, he cleared security, and then departed the building. He had prayed hard, hoping to end this deception today. But Talbot's refusal to end the assignment proved his prayers had been denied. Decisively.

Indefinitely.

Talbot's word speared through Grant but it was Dayton's suspicions, the odd look in his eyes when they spoke about Crawford, that most worried Grant. Was that because something was there? Or because Madison had planted doubts in his mind about Crawford being silenced before he could recant his confessions and her relating that to Talbot and Dayton?

Unsure, Grant pulled his keys from his pocket, and made his way across the parking lot.

Indefinitely.

Infiltrating Lost, Inc., had made sense—at one point. But why keep a plant in place on a closed case where everyone had been cleared? That didn't make sense… unless Talbot or Dayton doubted Crawford's guilt. But why would they? And why not just tell Grant they had doubts? He was Talbot's hand-chosen investigator, after all.

Grant paused to let a blue truck pass between the rows of parked cars. What had happened in there made no sense, neither their orders nor their conduct. Talbot's warning to Grant to keep his eyes and ears open…that look in his eye. Was it a warning, too? And the way Talbot had looked at Dayton. What was that all about? The truck passed and Grant walked on. Halfway to his car, he stopped dead in his tracks between a black sedan and a white SUV. His stomach clenched. There was one situation where their orders and conduct made perfect sense.

If Madison was right.

But she couldn't be right. Talbot and Dayton involved in two murders? That was insane.

Wasn't it?

Unsure, Grant got into his Jeep and headed off the base. As soon as he cleared the gate, he dialed Madison.

She answered on the second ring. "Hi, Grant."

He'd never heard Madison McKay sound so…open. Unguarded even. "What's wrong with you?"

"Nothing at all. Why? Where are you?"

Not quite sure about this shift in her, he reserved judgment. "On my way back to the office. Are you there, or at home?"

"Actually, I just picked up my dress for the ball tonight—it's totally gorgeous—and now I'm heading home for a nap so I don't wear a gorgeous gown with dark bags under my eyes."

Gearing up for the ball, or for more surveillance after it? "I've been thinking about our talk this morning and what you said about Crawford."

"And?"

"It makes sense. Even if he killed Beth Crane, why would he wait so long to take out Pace?"

"Pace wasn't a threat until later," she told Grant. "After Beth was killed, Brett Lund, the WKME station manager, dropped the assignment. He didn't pick it up again for three years."

"When he assigned the story to Pace."

"That's right. Until then, Pace didn't know a thing about any of it."

Grant pulled into a drive-through Starbucks and ordered coffee, then asked, "Why did Lund wait? Why would he sit on a huge story for three years?"

"Don't I wish I knew? Lund died before answering that question, but I've thought about it, and the only thing that stands up to scrutiny is that after Beth was killed, Lund was scared stiff. He had a wife and two kids, you know."

"That only works if Lund connected Beth Crane's murder to her inquiries about the Nest. He'd have had to know she wasn't killed in a home invasion like everyone believed until Crawford confessed." Beth's husband, Ian Crane, had been a doctor. Everyone in North Bay knew it. But anyone who knew Ian Crane knew he didn't keep so much as an aspirin at home to protect Beth. So the police had deduced Beth's murder had been by a random stranger—until Crawford confessed.

"Lund made the connection between Beth and Talbot and/or Dayton and the Nest. He admitted as much to Ian." Blaming himself for Beth's death, Ian had stopped practicing medicine to hire on with Madison and devote himself to finding Beth's killer. He and Madison's best friend, Maggie Mason, had worked together and gone through struggles of their own, but this past Christmas, they had worked through them and fallen in love. What an adventure that had been, going up against serial killer Gary Crawford!

"When did Lund admit the connection?"

"Right before he shot himself." Madison sighed. "They talked in his office. He admitted to Ian and Maggie that he knew Beth had been murdered and he feared for his family so he'd kept his mouth shut. When nothing happened to him and three years passed, Lund thought it was safe to check out the case, so he pulled the records and assigned David Pace."

"So then, like Beth, Pace goes to the commander for confirmation on the Nest, and shortly thereafter, he's killed."

"Right," Madison said. "Minutes after Ian left the meeting, Lund got a phone call—the records have been scrubbed so we don't know from whom—and then shot himself."

He'd made the connection, all right, and he'd sacrificed David Pace for the story. And that's why Madison was so invested in this case. "Pace didn't know about Beth, did he?"

"According to his wife, no."

"And what happened to his records on the case?"

"Detective Cray took a look at them. He saw nothing to indicate Pace knew Beth even existed."

This must have nearly knocked Ian to his knees. He'd looked for his wife's murderer for three years, and then to discover this? Poor guy.

"Grant? Did you hear me?"

"What? Sorry. I was thinking about how hard learning this had to have been on Ian."

"Very."

Neither he nor Maggie had said much about Crawford or the security breach, for that matter. "What did you say that I missed?"

"I said," Madison repeated, "something seems different. What's happened to you?"

No way could he answer that question. He wished he could tell her the truth, but he didn't have that luxury. All he could do was play dumb and stick as close to the truth as possible. But inside the battle raged between truth and lies, right and wrong, his head and heart, and betrayal and loyalty. He could follow the dictates of his faith, be loyal to his country, or be loyal to her. He couldn't be all three, and that grated at him on so many levels it'd take a lifetime to list them all. And he feared she'd hate him forever for deceiving her. "What do you mean?"

"You sound almost as if you're hearing what I'm saying for the first time."

He grunted. Maybe he was. His perspective had changed. He was now entertaining the possibility she could be right.

"Are you coming around to my way of thinking?"

"I'm keeping an open mind." The woman was astute. He'd be foolish to forget it. "Take a nap. I'll pick you up at eight."

"Sorry. I won't be here."

Surprise rippled up his back. His hands tightened on the steering wheel. "What?"

"I have a date."

"I know. It's with me."

"I don't think so. My date is with the man who sent

me chocolates, a white stuffed teddy bear and a lovely card asking me to be his valentine."

"It arrived."

A lilt in her voice turned even more playful. "Oh, was that from you?"

"You know it was."

"Well, it all arrived just before I left the office to pick up my dress, but I couldn't tell who sent it because the card, while lovely, wasn't signed."

He'd agonized over how to sign it. Gone back and forth in his head and had nearly driven himself over the edge. Finally he'd just written her name on the envelope and at the top of the card and left it unsigned. He sipped at his coffee. "I was being mysterious to charm you."

"Well, you succeeded." A smile sounded in her voice. "I guess my date is with you, then. See you at eight—but meet me at the club. We have a little issue with the florist to resolve, so I need to be there early."

After ending the call, he set the phone down on the console and wondered what had gotten into her. Madison? Being playful? With *him?*

He liked her playful. He liked her regardless, but playful was…captivating.

Maybe he should keep her sleep deprived….

It could be his one shot to not lose her.

THREE

She took his breath away.

Madison's hair was up off her neck, but loose silver-blond strands fluttered around her face. He liked that. Her makeup was light—it was always light, except when she'd smeared her face with camo paint. Her dress was classic and vintage Madison: simple, elegant and a soft pastel that hinted at blue. The woman was a knockout.

What she saw in him, Grant couldn't imagine. But the tremor in her voice when in the car he'd talked about walking away from her told him he did matter. Maybe more than she realized.

That was good and bad. It ignited hope and despair in him, and probably in her, too. Why couldn't things between them be different? Personally, he wanted her to care. More than he dared admit to anyone but himself. This relationship had started out as an assignment, but one look at her had changed everything. They'd eased into dating, sharing meals after work, handling a bit of business on the weekend and letting it fold over into doing something fun together. Then before Christmas she'd started talking about the group cruise, and instead of *her* trip it became *their* trip.

He thought back, seeking a specific moment when they'd officially become a couple, or even started dating, but couldn't pinpoint one. Starting out, he'd sought every opportunity to be with her to spy on her—and she'd done the same thing with him. But now it seemed clear that spying had just given them permission to be together, which was what they both wanted anyway. At least, that's how their relationship had developed for him, and he believed it had for her, as well. He couldn't pinpoint the exact moment his feelings for her had gotten personal. But he remembered vividly the instant he'd realized it.

They'd been on the cruise, caught in a hurricane, and Maggie Mason had been in trouble and needed Madison. She'd done everything humanly possible to get off that ship and get home to her friend. And watching her efforts, it hit him hard that he wanted her to care that much about him. To want to move mountains to get to him because he needed her. And in that same instant he knew he did care about her that much, and if she needed him, he would move mountains to get to her.

Seconds later it hit just as hard that if Madison knew the truth she would feel as betrayed by him as she'd been by her superiors. That had thrown him into the tailspin of his life.

Sometimes even a man of faith had no choice. He didn't want to deceive her and would give his right arm to not do it, but he was powerless. A direct order was a direct order, and an oath was an oath. When he made a vow, he kept it. He was either a man of honor or he wasn't. He prayed hard and often and made every effort to do the right thing on all sides, though he'd be shocked if Madison saw it that way. The one woman who knocked him to his knees would walk out of his life for good.

Their relationship and situation was that simple and that complex, as Madison liked to say.

Still, standing in the club's ballroom looking at her, laughing with Paul Mason and his new wife, Della, and chatting with Paul's sister Maggie and her soon-to-be husband, Ian Crane, the widower of Beth Crane, Madison looked happy. Content. At peace with her world.

She wasn't, and until she made her peace with her past, she wouldn't be. She was a woman of faith, but right now that faith was hampered by her bitterness at being sacrificed. When she said her superiors had sacrificed her, she meant her military superiors had betrayed her, but she also meant she felt betrayed by God for not sparing her when taken POW. It had taken Grant a while to figure that out.

In his curled palm he rolled over the last of the gifts he'd gotten her for Valentine's Day: a stone. Hopefully, sometime tonight he'd feel that his heart was in the right place to give it to her. If not, he'd hang on to it and pray hard a right time came. But first he had to get his breath back.

She caught sight of him and smiled.

And left him breathless all over again.

* * *

The ballroom at North Bay Country Club had been transformed into a romantic wonderland, filled with red roses, little twinkling lights and tall columns that stretched ceiling to floor framing the stage and dance floor. Madison glanced from strategically placed foliage to draped lengths of fabric that formed areas for couples to chat.

Spotting Grant, she stopped speaking midsentence, unprepared for the impact of seeing him in his mess dress.

"I do believe you're speechless."

Maggie's amused remark jerked Madison down out of the clouds. "I am not. But he sure cleans up nice." In street clothes, Grant always had women take a second look, but in his mess dress they stopped, stared and even gawked.

"Sure does." Maggie chuckled. "This looks good on you."

"Oh, you like the dress? I found it at—"

"Not the dress, though it's pretty. Love."

Madison broke gazes with Grant, and glared at her lifelong friend. "Love? Are you crazy?"

Maggie hiked her chin. "Okay, then."

"It's not love," Madison insisted, feeling her face heat. "I—I just like him."

"Liking is good." Maggie slid Ian a glance he missed. "Love's better."

Madison shot her another you've-lost-your-mind glare, then walked over to Grant.

He slowly perused her. “Nice dress.”

“Thanks.” The band on the stage started playing a waltz.

“May I have this dance?” His eyes twinkled.

Her gran had told her a thousand times. *When it comes to men, hon, their eyes are windows straight to their souls.* And Grant’s gaze spoke volumes about his feelings for her. Suddenly shy, something she’d never been in her life, Madison remembered her promise to take a leap of faith. *Just until he does anything to cross me.* She stepped into Grant’s arms and into trust.

They danced and talked quietly of little nothings, and as she let herself get lost in his arms, for the first time since returning from Afghanistan, she forgot to be bitter or angry or to feel the sting of betrayal.

As the evening wore on, they chatted with friends, others from the agency and local officials. Just before midnight, Madison glanced from the dance floor to the door and saw Commander Talbot and Vice Commander Dayton walk in. Their attendance at North Bay functions was a normal part of the military’s community relations, yet still she tensed.

“It’s all right,” Grant said, not missing a step. “They come to everything. You know that.”

She did, but it still troubled her. Especially when Talbot walked straight over to Mrs. Renault.

“Renée, it’s wonderful to see you.”

“You, too, Andrew.” She craned her neck and accepted his kiss to her cheek. “How have you been?”

He answered, and then invited her to dance. She

joined him and they did a Viennese waltz that looked polished and practiced, and Madison wondered just how many times before they had danced together.

"Striking couple, aren't they?" Grant asked.

They were. And it irritated Madison because she didn't trust the man. But was that fair? Could the man looking at Mrs. Renault with such genuine tenderness be capable of cold-blooded murder? Madison just wasn't sure. The scent of all the red roses suddenly seemed cloying. She whispered to Grant, "Let's walk down to the gazebo."

"You okay?"

"Fine. I just need some air and I love it down there."

They went outside through the broad French doors, then walked in silence between tall white columns that stretched over a wide expanse of perfectly manicured lawn and down the walkway to the boardwalk at the water's edge. It ended at an ornate gazebo. Once under its roof, Madison drew in a deep breath, inhaling the tangy scent of salt water in the air. The night was chilly, but not cold.

"I see now why Maggie painted this place for you—the painting in your office. The expression on your face is pure bliss."

Madison nodded, a smile curving her lips. "It's one of my favorite places in the whole world."

Grant looked around, skimming the shoreline, the cove, the houses on the far side. "What's special about it?"

To him it probably looked no different than many

other coves in the area. But she saw something here he didn't. She grinned at him and took two steps left. "My first kiss happened just about here."

Grant frowned. "I don't think I want to walk down that particular memory lane, since you weren't kissing me."

"I was eleven." Madison laughed. "I attended social graces lessons here. Gilbert Moss was my partner, and I thought he was the most amazing boy I'd ever met in my life."

"Why?"

"Between you and me, he always wore a suit. I discovered I had a real thing for cute boys in ties."

Grant laughed. "Wearing a tie got him an 'amazing,' huh? Lucky boy."

"Not really." Sadness flooded her. "Gilbert quit the class the day before our debut gathering. I didn't participate much, not having a partner, and I wasn't too happy with him. I came out here and remembered how happy I was the evening he kissed me and..."

"You were less upset with him." When she nodded, he went on. "So when you need to feel happy—or grounded or need a change of attitude—this is where you come."

She nodded. "That's why Maggie gave me the painting. So I'd feel grounded and happy in my office."

"She's a good friend." He stepped closer to her. "Did seeing Mrs. Renault with the commander upset you that much?"

"No. Mrs. Renault can handle him just fine." A little gust of wind teased her hair. She brushed it from her face, and tilted her head. If she was going to trust him, this was that moment. Madison studied his face, saw good in it, and trusting the twinkle, took the leap. "The truth is, you upset me."

He sighed. "What did I do now?"

"No, that came out wrong." She placed a hand on his forearm. "I meant, what I feel for you upsets me."

"That's hardly better…or is it?" He frowned. "What exactly do you feel, Madison?"

"A lot more than I'd like," she admitted. "But I made myself a promise and I'm going to keep it." She uncurled her hand. "This doesn't have a pretty card with it, and there's no shiny wrapping or bow, but it carries its own charm and it is precious to me. I want you to have it, Grant."

He looked into her open palm, and surprise spilled over from his face to his voice. "Your Purple Heart medal?"

Madison swallowed hard, and nodded. "It's a symbol of my affection for you…and of my trust."

He didn't move.

"Don't you want it?"

Grant lifted his gaze to hers, and the storm raging within him reflected in his eyes. "More than anything."

She bobbed her hand. "Then take it."

He raised his hand, but didn't touch the medal. "Are you sure? I know what this means to you. Are you really sure you want me to have it?"

His hunger for what stood behind the gift showed

in every tense line on his face, in his rigid stance. He wanted her to want him to have it badly. And that yearning chiseled away yet another chink in the armor around her heart. It crumbled and fell away. "I'm positive," she said and meant it. "I decided today that I'd been looking at us all wrong. I should trust you until I have reason not to. That's fair. That's right."

"Madison, you know this is complicated…."

His oath. His requirement to report on activities at her agency. Well, she had nothing to hide there. Her trek to the perimeter of the Nest, yes, and Grant could hurt her if he reported it. But if he had reported it—and if he thought she'd find anything that shouldn't be found, he would have reported it—she already would have been hauled in and in serious trouble with Commander Talbot. "I know it's complicated, but I want to give you—us—a chance. It's taken me a while, but I've finally gotten there."

He smiled, clearly bemused.

She smiled back and leaned in, then gently kissed him.

A long moment later, Grant looked down at her, dragged his fingertips down her jaw. "You take my breath away."

"The feeling is mutual." She smiled up at him.

He reached into his pocket and pulled out a pink object. "I have something for you, too."

In the moonlight she saw that it was an oblong, flat pink stone. Something was written on it. *Trust.* "It's a worry stone," he told her. "You rub it when you're tense or worried. I thought you'd like that."

She did. "Does it help?"

"I hope what it means will." He lifted her chin so she looked him in the eye. "I've carried that stone my entire military career—to keep me grounded—and I'm giving it to you. This is a reminder."

Confusing. "Of what?"

Urgency filled his voice. "That no matter how things look or seem, you should always trust your instincts."

A warning. One that burned as clearly in his eyes as in his words.

A warning that chilled her to the bone.

The Valentine's Day ball wound down after midnight and just after one in the morning, Madison returned to her office, quickly changed into her black hoodie and smeared her face with camouflage paint, then headed out to the Nest.

Her emotions were in turmoil. *Trust your instincts.* Grant had clearly been warning her about something. About him? Was he telling her to trust her innate responses on everything? Or that now he, too, thought Talbot and/or Dayton had killed Beth Crane and David Pace?

The uncertainty was frightening. He'd taken the Purple Heart and she had replaced it with his pink rubbing stone as her talisman to stay focused on her mission. *Trust.* Funny, she thought, sprinting through the woods. His warning should have her breaking out in hives, but it didn't. It felt protective, and the leap of faith she had taken on him deepened. And to trust a man she was attracted to and cared for, whether or not she wanted to, felt good. Better than good.

When she reached the fence, she lay flat on the ground and positioned her binoculars. The guards stood with their backs to the buildings as they had the night before, about twenty feet apart and armed to the teeth. This definitely was not a readiness exercise. Installations functioned under the THREATCON System and its levels ranged from Alpha to Delta. Each level carried a corresponding set of measures, policies and procedures. The Nest, being isolated and confined to a small need-to-know loop, typically stood at THREATCON Alpha, but the signs were all evident they had activated the measures under Bravo. The threat might be specific or general, but the commander expected trouble.

A crunching sound came from her distant left. She stilled, listened intently.

Crackle. Crunch. Snap.

Definitely footsteps…and they were getting closer.

Springing to a crouch, she strained to see with and without her binoculars and saw no one, but twigs continued to snap, leaves crush. Whoever it was either wasn't proficient at stealth maneuvers or didn't care about being overheard. She turned to run and snagged her hoodie on a spiny bush. The fabric ripped.

The tearing sounded like a blast in the darkness. Whoever was tramping through the woods would catch her for sure. The footsteps came closer, faster.

Her heart raced. Whether or not they knew she was there, she couldn't tell, but she didn't dare hang around to find out. She tore the hoodie loose from its snag, and then ran through the woods toward her point of entry.

Images of Afghanistan and the night of her capture flashed through her mind. She'd run then, too, and found herself surrounded by a dozen armed men. She'd failed to evade them, and feared she'd fail again now. Blood surging through her, pounding in her ears, she pushed back against the memories, trying hard to focus only on now, this moment, but the capture images persisted, creating a jumbled tangle of then and now. *Stop it! Stop!* She forced herself to stay in the moment, to keep running.

When she made it back to her Jag and got in, she quickly locked the doors and took off, gasping in air. She wished Grant were here, sitting in her passenger seat, even if it meant he'd be searing her ears with a lecture and asking her for promises to stay away from the Nest. Promises she couldn't make and wouldn't keep.

But Grant wasn't there.

Whatever came, she'd face it alone. *God, help me. I can't do this again on my own. Help me.*

When she pulled into her own garage and the door shut behind her, she drew her first easy breath. For a long moment she couldn't seem to move, so she just sat there, slumped over the wheel, thanking God for protecting her and getting her safely home.

Calmer, she removed the ignition key, saw how badly

her hand was shaking and covered her eyes. "You're fine. It's all okay," she told herself. "You're safe."

In her office at ten o'clock the next morning, Madison discovered everything was not fine.

A brash young lieutenant walked into her office unannounced. "Ms. McKay?" he asked.

Startled, she looked up from her paperwork and into the soldier's ruddy face. "Yes?" Where was Mrs. Renault? Why hadn't she intercepted him? "Are you in the habit of walking into offices uninvited, Lieutenant?"

"I didn't see anyone." He didn't meet her gaze.

The name tag above his pocket read *Blake.*

Mrs. Renault suddenly appeared at the doorway behind Blake, her expression stern. Madison lifted her chin, warning her not to make her presence known. "In that case, my apologies. What do you want, Lieutenant Blake?"

"Commander Talbot sent me, ma'am."

Madison's heart jackhammered. Why hadn't Talbot just picked up the phone? "For what purpose?"

"He ordered me to escort you to his office."

Mrs. Renault's slight nod warned Madison to be amiable.

Madison forced herself to smile. She stood up. "Well, I'd better grab my purse and follow you over there, then."

"I'll drive you, ma'am." He shifted on his feet. "Talbot's orders."

Whatever this was about, it would play out far better

for her to seem cooperative. With Mrs. Renault aware of what was happening, cooperation couldn't hurt and might help. "How thoughtful of him. I guess you'll drive me back as well—or will I need to phone someone to retrieve me?"

His face turned ruddy. "The commander didn't say, ma'am."

That worried her even more. Mrs. Renault stepped away from the doorway so the soldier wouldn't see her. Where was Grant? Had he reported her to Talbot after all? Her heart hurt. *No. Please no.* Trusting him at all had been so hard and it had seemed to go well. She'd actually been relaxed and happy and…not bitter. "Very well. Just let me tell my assistant—"

"I'm sorry, Ms. McKay. The commander specifically asked that you not tell anyone where you're going."

So she was supposed to be sitting in her office one minute and vanished the next. How convenient for them—and how badly this boded for her. Her heart beat harder, faster, threatening to take out her chest wall and break her ribs. "I see. This isn't an invitation—it's a command performance."

The lieutenant didn't answer.

He didn't have to. No car, no driving herself, no way home… It was a command performance, all right. And all signs pointed to it being a testy one. But Grant couldn't be involved. She'd seen the twinkle in his eye. She'd dared to trust him. She'd given him her Purple Heart and he knew what it meant to her and had accepted it. He couldn't have betrayed her.

So what was this about, then?

The man in the woods. Had whoever had been out by the Nest last night actually seen her?

She would have said no, definitely not. Even aided with night vision gear, she hadn't seen that person.

But now, she wasn't so sure.

"Madison, thank you for coming." Commander Talbot rose to his feet and motioned to a visitor's chair on the opposite side of his imposing desk.

There were no windows in his office. For security purposes, that was common for high-level officers, and she'd mentally prepared herself for it, but the absence of daylight still gave her that confined feeling she'd endured in the cell in Afghanistan. That same cold, clammy feeling that threatened to steal away her breath. His office was sterile—smelled of cleaner, and nothing was out of place, nor were there any personal items. "I could hardly resist such a charming invitation, Commander."

He had the grace to look away. "I'm sorry if my tactics offended, but I needed to get you here immediately."

"Quietly, too, apparently. I couldn't even let Mrs. Renault know I was leaving?" Hopefully, his feelings toward her would carry over to Madison. He knew how close they were; everyone did. "Why?"

Behind her, someone walked into the office and the commander fell silent. She looked over and saw Vice Commander Dayton, carrying a neon-orange file. He opened it on the corner of the commander's desk. "May I?" he asked Talbot.

The commander's expression tensed and he gave Dayton a curt nod.

What was going on here? Talbot looked wary and worried. Dayton looked like a cocky conqueror. Both were making her feel like stalked prey. Her skin crawled. "I don't mean to be ungracious, Commander, but I do have a business to run, so if we could—"

Dayton cut her off. "Where were you last night, Ms. McKay?"

"Why?" Her whereabouts were truly none of his business and she had every right to demand civility or to ignore him.

Dayton gave her a warning look. "This can be a pleasant exchange or a not-so-pleasant exchange. I'm up for either."

"As am I." She smiled at him.

He got the message, but Talbot interceded. "We've had another security incident, Madison."

Dayton took the cue. "We would appreciate it if you'd tell us where you were last night."

Much better. "I was at the Valentine's ball at the country club. Commander Talbot was there—he can attest to it."

Dayton looked at Talbot, who nodded.

"And after the ball?" Dayton's civility slid.

She dipped her chin, looked up at him. "I'm hearing an accusation in your tone. Need I remind you that I've already agreed to cooperate?"

He masked his expression, reached into the file and removed an evidence bag, then held it up. "Does this look familiar?"

Too familiar. A piece of torn fabric was inside the clear bag. Her hoodie fabric that had gotten snagged on the bush.

Lieutenant Blake knocked at the door, walked in and handed Dayton a larger plastic bag. "Retrieved from the bath adjacent to her office, sir," he said. "Mrs. Renault photographed it and made me sign for it."

"Excellent." Dayton smiled, but there was no warmth in it.

The hoodie. They had her dead to rights.

"Does Mrs. Renault know Madison is here?" Dayton asked Blake.

"No, sir. No one knows where she is. Mrs. Renault assumed she'd gone to Miss Addie's Café for breakfast."

Madison's relief was palpable. Mrs. Renault did know, but if she'd admitted it to Blake, no doubt she, too, would have been hauled in. She said a silent prayer of thanks for her friend's silence.

Their intentions were not yet clear, but one thing was certain.

She was definitely in trouble.

At headquarters Grant sat at the far end of the conference-room table. Only he and the commander were in the room, though why Talbot had summoned Grant here rather than to the commander's office, he had no idea.

When Talbot turned on the white noise machine that prevented anyone outside the room from hearing what was said inside it, Grant's nerve endings started buzzing. Whatever this was about, it was bad news.

"Grant, we've got a situation." The commander paced alongside the conference table, clearly agitated. "I've had to detain Madison McKay."

"Detain her?" Grant's heart beat wild as a drum. "Why?"

Talbot stopped two feet from Grant's chair. "Did you know that she was spying on the Nest?"

Oh, no. "Sir?"

"Look, I know you've developed feelings for the woman, but I don't have time for games. She's spying on the Nest from its perimeter in the woods. Did you know it?"

There it was. The direct question he'd most dreaded. "She's not spying on the Nest, Commander. She's looking for evidence on a case that has nothing to do with the Nest as an entity."

"What case? What kind of evidence?"

Grant met the commander's eyes. "Madison believes you or Dayton had Beth Crane and David Pace killed for asking about the Nest."

"What?"

"Their sources were accurate on the information leaked." Grant lifted a hand.

Talbot stilled, shut his eyes a brief moment, and when he reopened them, resignation slid down over his face. "I should have known."

“Excuse me, sir?”

“When I refused to release the satellite images on David Pace’s car, I should have known that she wouldn’t just let it rest until I did. I should have known that she’d dismiss Gary Crawford’s confessions—they’re what tagged him as Blue Shoes, the murderer—and I should have anticipated that she’d suspect he was a fraud and Dayton or I was the real Blue Shoes.”

Before Crawford confessed, Blue Shoes was the moniker the authorities had adopted for David Pace’s murderer. Someone had put neon-blue aquatic shoes on him postmortem. The blue shoes had been seen before in other cases. When Crawford confessed, Blue Shoes’s identity was resolved…or so everyone had thought. Now, Grant wasn’t sure what to think about Blue Shoes, Crawford or about the commander.

Talbot returned to pacing. “I believed she would trust me.”

“Madison?” He had to know better. “Sir, she doesn’t trust anyone.” Well, she was trusting Grant now—at least, she had been. But with Talbot detaining her, she likely didn’t trust Grant anymore. She probably thought he’d turned her in.

Detained.

The magnitude of her situation bore down on him. She could vanish forever. His heart rebelled.

“She trusts Renée Renault, and I thought since Renée trusts me, Madison would, too,” Talbot said, then paused and stared at Grant. “Madison does trust Renée, doesn’t she?”

"Yes, sir." What exactly was Talbot saying? "Why would Madison need to trust you?"

Sadness joined disappointment and worry and the three warred in Talbot's eyes. "For the moment, let's just say if she had, she wouldn't be detained."

"But she *is* detained."

"Yes."

Anger churned in Grant. He'd warned her to stay away from the Nest. Why hadn't she listened to him? "Where?"

"In a bunker cellblock at the Nest."

Grant's stomach twisted and his chest went tight. "Sir, you know she was a POW. We left her in an Afghan cell for eighteen months. She can't stand being confined in any way. You know what this will do to her. You can't—"

Talbot lifted a hand. "She left me no choice."

Grant took a moment to get his temper controlled, then looked from the white wall back at the commander. His emotions remained in riot. "She's a civilian."

"I'm aware of that." Talbot's voice rose. "I'm also aware that the evidence against her for spying on the facility is overwhelming. She once had access here at the installation and at the Nest. Have you forgotten that?"

"She had limited access."

"And full knowledge that all Nest operations are classified."

"But her interest wasn't in the Nest, per se."

"How do you know that beyond a reasonable doubt?" Talbot shook his head. "We're talking treason here,

Grant." He lifted a warning finger. "Be careful you don't let your heart rule your head."

Treason? Grant stood up. "Sir, Madison McKay would never commit treason. I know it." He pulled her Purple Heart medal from his pocket. "This proves it. It means the world to her. She'd never violate it by leaking anything about the Nest, and she'd never double-cross her country. No way."

"You said it yourself, Grant. We left her behind. That's directed the entire course of her life. Don't you know that's what Lost, Inc., is all about?"

"Yes, sir, I do know. She is angry and bitter at what we did. Not about being left—that she understands. But because her parents were told she was dead, and it brought them so much pain. That's the truth of it. Fault her for being bitter about that and no one on our side dirtying their hands to help her return to the States after she escaped, but don't accuse her of treason. She is not guilty of it."

"Evidence doesn't lie. We have images of her in the woods, watching the Nest through binoculars. And fabric torn from a sweatshirt that's indisputably hers was found on a branch near the perimeter."

"I'm not disputing she was there," Grant told him. "I'm disputing that she was committing treason." His career hung on his next statement. "You know it as well as I do, and you know what detaining her will do to her, yet—"

"I know what Madison's been through, but I have

an obligation to protect the interests of the nation, I—" He stopped suddenly. "I have to do what I have to do."

The man was clearly conflicted, and that confused Grant. Talbot always seemed to know exactly what he was doing and why he was doing it. His uncertainty fueled Grant's own. Was Talbot detaining Madison for an alternative reason? Maybe to protect her? But from what danger? "You won't harm her." When Talbot didn't answer, Grant swallowed hard and reminded him, "Anything happens to her and Mrs. Renault will never forgive you. She looks at Madison—"

"Like a daughter." He dragged a hand through his thin hair. "I'm aware of that. But Renée has no reason to blame me. She doesn't know Madison is here."

Everything in Grant rebelled. "What are you going to do to her?"

Talbot frowned. "Whatever I must do to fulfill my duty."

Grant tried to wrap his mind around all this. He couldn't decide whether Talbot had detained her to prosecute or protect her. "What exactly are you telling me, Commander?"

He frowned, stuffed his hands into his pockets. "I'm telling you I am not Blue Shoes." He dropped the heel of a fisted hand onto the gleaming conference-room table. "Oh, but it grates at my soul to have to defend myself. Thirty years of service, and my integrity is in question with those I've trusted implicitly. Do you realize how degrading and infuriating that is?"

"I don't, no. But it's probably about as degrading

and infuriating as serving your country, being held as a POW and abandoned, escaping and getting home, then devoting your life to helping the lost return home and being accused of treason. I expect Madison could relate well."

Grant accepted the glare that remark earned him without comment, and he reserved judgment on Talbot's guilt or innocence. Maybe he wasn't Blue Shoes. Maybe he was. The jury was still out on that one.

Innocent until proven guilty was a luxury afforded only in the civilian world. In the military, you were assumed guilty until proven innocent. Considering the potential for disaster and possible consequences to legions of citizens, that was the way things had to work. "Commander, are you telling me Madison is right? That you're not Blue Shoes so Dayton must be, and he killed David Pace and Beth Crane?"

Talbot's face leaked its color and all emotion left him. The man was now buried, leaving only the commander. "I'm saying I don't believe Crawford is Blue Shoes."

"Are you convinced Dayton *isn't?*"

A muscle in his cheek twitched. Talbot clamped his jaw. "Dayton is my vice, Grant."

He hadn't answered the question. Not condemning his second-in-command, but he sure hadn't defended him. Did that mean he truly believed Dayton was innocent? Or was Talbot just following protocol—guilty until proven innocent?

Only he knew, and clearly he had revealed all he

intended to on the matter. Given no choice, Grant accepted that, and moved on. "You're afraid the real Blue Shoes will come after Madison."

Concern flickered in Talbot's eyes, then deepened and poured over into his voice. "Aren't you?"

"Frankly, I don't know what to think."

The commander shared specifics about the evidence against Madison, ending with, "There's no doubt she was spying on the Nest. We have her on camera. There's no disputing the physical evidence."

There wasn't.

"But her motivation will factor," Talbot said. "So while that's significant, it's not what troubles me most."

How could there possibly be more? Grant was already mentally staggering.

Talbot worried his lower lip, studied Grant a long moment, sizing him up, then added, "Early this morning I received a briefing that made getting Madison here quickly critical. A call from the warden at the Florida State Prison."

Chills raced up and down Grant's spine. "Crawford?"

Talbot nodded. "About four this morning, Gary Crawford was found murdered in his jail cell."

Grant absorbed the shock. Madison's warning replayed in his mind. She'd said that if Talbot or Dayton were guilty of murdering Pace and Crane, then Gary Crawford would be killed to silence him. She'd said the commanders wouldn't risk Crawford recanting his confessions. At the time, Grant had thought if she was right, Crawford's days were numbered.

And they had been.

So Madison had been right about Crawford. Did that make her right about Talbot or Dayton? Or did they have a different suspect on their hands?

"I've restricted access to Madison," Talbot said, interrupting Grant's thoughts. "No one is permitted near her except you and Major Beecher."

"Me?" Shock streaked up Grant's back. "But, sir, she probably thinks I turned her in to you. She's not going to cooperate with me." And why Beecher? He was an explosives specialist. He wasn't… Wait. Talbot trusted him. He trusted them both.

"I said, only you and Beecher," Talbot repeated. "Do I need to make that a direct order, Major?"

Resignation seeped in and settled into his every cell. Any hope for Madison and him as a couple died. His heart ached, hollowed. "Yes, sir." Grant hiked his chin. "A direct order might help." If Dayton pushed to see her, Grant would need it.

"Then that's a direct order, Major. No one else gets close to Madison McKay—and I do mean no one."

Dayton. Maybe others. "I understand, sir."

Talbot's mask slid. "I am sorry, Grant. I know what it's like to care about someone and be in a…bad position."

Mrs. Renault. He didn't have to say her name for Grant to know what he meant. "Yes, sir." Grant stood up. "Is that it?"

"For now." Talbot lifted his chin. "Report to the cell-block. Major Beecher is manning it now. You two can work out a schedule—one of you stays with her all the time. He'll direct you to her."

"How long will she be detained?" That would be the first question out of her mouth—after she stopped screaming at Grant for betraying her. Would she even hear his explanations? Doubtful.

"Indefinitely."

FOUR

Madison stood in the middle of her six-by-eight jail cell. She'd been blindfolded and guided here and only when inside the cell had the blindfold been removed.

That's when the panic really started. She'd done every relaxation exercise she'd ever learned and, while the images of her cell in Afghanistan weren't bleeding into the images of this one anymore, the feelings she'd had at being held against her will had returned full force.

A narrow cot, a toilet behind a short cinder-block wall. Nothing else. Not one other thing in this cell. She stared at the ceiling light—the old-type bare lightbulb—in the aisle between the two long rows of cells and tried to comfort herself. No scorpions or spiders, no crushing heat. This space was climate controlled, a comfortable seventy-five degrees, and the large grate embedded in the white ceiling was a potent reminder that this was not Afghanistan. Even at night her Afghan cell had been hot and the ceiling had been rock, the floor dirt and hard, not tiled. No natural light penetrated into this cell or slanted down the center, no fresh air flowed in from outside. The bars were heavy steel, not wood. This cell had to be in a vault above ground… or in an underground bunker.

That realization sobered her. *Please, don't let it be at the Nest. Please.*

So far, she'd spotted two cameras fixed in her direction. Talbot's minions were watching her every move. She refused to pace or to give in to fear. Mrs. Renault knew she was here. She'd do something. She'd tell Grant—she'd brought him out to the Nest, hadn't she? He'd do something…if he hadn't helped put her in here.

Had he been playing her for a fool all along, worming his way into her heart to get her to trust him, only to betray her?

No. He'd accepted her Purple Heart.

She took in three deep breaths, then let them out slowly and rubbed her arms, chasing away the goose bumps that peppered her flesh. Believing the worst about Grant would be so easy. As easy as it had been to be bitter with God for not sparing her the experience of being a POW. Maybe she needed the wisdom gained then for what was happening now? God had deserved better than bitterness. She prayed for forgiveness for not seeing that before now.

God and Grant deserved better than bitterness and distrust, and so did she. She wouldn't fall into that trap.

Yet Grant had warned her to trust her instincts. Had he meant for her not to trust him? Her thoughts flitted all over the place, bringing questions and doubts but no answers.

It had been hours since Dayton and Lieutenant Blake had slammed the cell door behind her. She hadn't seen a soul since then. This had to be the Nest. Where else would Talbot hold her and be certain no one else came around? Certainly not at the main installation's brig. It'd be bustling with activity. This cellblock was deserted, except for her. It had to be at a remote location, and nowhere was as remote as inside the Nest.

Maybe Mrs. Renault had already gone to Talbot to find out where Madison was and why she'd been brought in. Surely she had. What kind of reception would she get?

Not knowing, Madison didn't even know what to pray for on this. Talbot, and not Dayton, had ordered her detained. Would going to him be a wise or foolish move? Clueless, she lifted her gaze toward the ceiling. *The greater good, God. I don't know what help I need, but You do. I—I—*

Footsteps sounded in the aisle. "Madison."

She looked down and through the bars, stunned silent. *Grant?* He was the last person she expected to see here—and the last person she *wanted* to see.

Betrayed.

He searched her face. "Are you all right?"

Madison didn't answer. She couldn't. Grant. *Here?* He knew not only about the Nest but stood deep within its bowels—where else could this be—and he was wearing his military uniform. The truth slammed into her. *Traitor.* Betrayal stung her again and pain sliced through her heart "You lied to me."

"Yes." He flinched, his eyes shining overly bright. "As little as possible," he said. "I couldn't tell you." He mouthed, *You're being monitored.* He shifted his gaze left, then right.

She'd already pegged the two cameras aimed at her cell from the center aisle ceiling and blinked once. He'd recognize her *Yes* response.

Logically, she knew he'd had to keep his active-duty status from her, but it didn't do a thing to make her feel better. She turned her back to him and the cameras. "Was it all a lie?" When he didn't answer, she looked back over her shoulder at him.

No. He again mouthed the word, keeping his back to the cameras' watchful lenses. He stepped closer to the bars, shielding his hand with his body. "Do you need anything?" He wiggled his fingertip, motioned her closer.

She stepped up to the bars. "Water would be good." He pressed something through the bars. Her Purple Heart.

Tears threatened. She sucked in a sharp breath.

Look at it later, he silently mouthed.

Again she blinked. She pulled the pink rubbing stone out of her pocket, tried to pass it to him. That Major Beecher had let her keep it surprised her. It was the first bit of good anything that had happened today.

"Keep it." Grant refused to take it.

He still trusted her, and wordlessly reiterated his

warning to her to trust her instincts. She slipped both the medal and the stone into her pocket.

"Have you eaten?"

This wasn't natural. It wasn't normal. Her feelings were so jumbled she didn't know whether to kiss him or knock his lights out. "You owe me an explanation."

"The only one I can give you, you won't like."

"I'd like to hear it anyway."

Regret flashed through his eyes. "Orders, Madison. You wore the uniform. You know how it is."

She did. And that he took no pleasure in deceiving her was clear. But could she trust her reading of a man who'd thoroughly and completely deceived her? "You knew how much trust mattered to me. You knew, and you took my medal anyway. How could you do that to me?"

"I did what I had to do. You know how these things work." He grabbed the bars, curled his fingers around them until his fingertips turned white. "Step into my shoes. What would you have done?"

"I don't want to step into your shoes. I took a leap of faith on you, and it was hard, but I did it. And now—splat. That's what I got for trusting you."

She stepped away, turned her back to him. "Just go away, Grant. I don't want to see you right now. I don't know if I ever want to see you again."

"It'll take a while for you to come to grips with this," he said. When she didn't respond, he whispered, "Madison, look at me. Please."

She tried and failed to hide her pain but glanced sideward at him anyway. The urge to cry overwhelmed her. She bit down on her tongue to hold back the tears. He would not get that, too.

The regret in his voice touched his eyes. Again he silently mouthed a message. *Crawford is dead. Murdered. Trust your instincts.* Aloud, he repeated, "Have you eaten?"

Her heart threatened to shoot out of her chest. Her pulse throbbed in her temples. Crawford was dead. They'd killed him. That meant she was the only one left seeking the truth, and now they had removed her as an obstacle. Would they kill her, too? "No, I haven't eaten today."

"I'll get you some lunch."

"You're guarding me?" She let out an exasperated sigh. "Of all people, you?"

"Me and Major Beecher. One or the other of us will be with you at all times. No one else."

"Why do I need constant monitoring?" She threw up her hands. "I'm in a locked cell with no windows, underground, in a facility few know exists. Where exactly am I supposed to go?"

"Nowhere." He mouthed, *Think.*

Confirmed. She was inside the Nest. Lord, help her. Confused about Grant and totally out of sorts, she stilled. The threatening tears burned the back of her nose and crept toward her eyes. Refusing to let him see her as weak, she turned her back to him. "Go away, Grant. Just go away."

He sighed. "I'll be back."

Should she take that as a threat or reassurance?

Unsure, she closed her eyes and squeezed the medal and stone in her pocket so hard she half expected them to fuse, and said not a word.

Major Beecher stood at the end of the corridor near the observation desk. "Well, she didn't take a swing at you. That's good news."

Grant grunted, clearly not happy with the situation.

"She was definitely shocked to see you." Beecher rubbed his full jaw, then folded his hands over his broad chest. "She had no idea you'd infiltrated her agency and were still active duty."

"She knew." Grant dropped into a swivel chair. "That I'd infiltrated Lost, Inc., anyway. She didn't know I was still active duty." He sighed again and pulled out his cell phone, dialed Miss Addie's Café and ordered Madison's favorite—chicken salad on whole wheat—and a Reuben for himself. He looked at Beecher. "Want anything?"

"Nah." Beecher lifted a brown bag. "Wait. Key lime pie."

Grant made it three, put it on his tab and said he'd have someone pick it up.

Beecher got on the phone and sent one of his guys out, then arranged to meet him in front of the outer facility's main headquarters building.

"Thanks." Grant stowed his phone. "Man, this is some kind of mess."

"It could be worse." Beecher glanced at the monitors.

Madison was the only person in the cellblock. That,

too, worried Grant. It would be irrationally easy to make her disappear. "How?"

"I could have shot her last night. What was she thinking, tromping in the woods like that?"

"You saw her?" Madison's stealth skills must be getting rusty.

"I heard her—well, I heard her sweatshirt tear. I didn't know what it was then. I made enough noise to warn anyone in a five-mile radius I was there but I didn't actually see her until she was in her Jag driving away."

The fabric sample found on the bush Talbot had shown him. "What do you think will happen to her?"

Worry and regret filled Beecher's eyes. "They don't have a lot of choice, Grant."

"She wasn't spying."

"She was—just maybe not for the reasons or with the intentions they first thought."

Beecher knew far more than Grant suspected he would. Talbot obviously had briefed him, too. "You know why she was out there?"

He nodded. "Not that it'll make any difference." Beecher looked over at the monitors.

Grant followed his gaze. Madison hadn't moved. Still stood with her back to the cameras in the center of her cell. Was she crying? He couldn't be sure, but why else would she stand so still for so long with her back turned?

Beecher pursed his lips and his close-cut hair caught the strong overhead light. "They wanted the David Pace case closed and forgotten. Except for her, it has been." He let out a little grunt. "They're not going to let her put a wrench in that. I can't see it happening."

Neither could Grant, which meant Madison could be stuck here forever.

"Better accept it." Beecher rocked back in his seat. "She'll probably never see the light of day again."

Every muscle in Grant's body contracted at once. Thinking it and hearing it said aloud were two different things. His stomach roiled. "That's not right."

"Or fair," Beecher agreed, hauling himself to his feet. "But it is what it is." He hitched his pants, then pulled his hat from where it had been tucked under his belt and seated it on his head. "I'm going to pick up lunch. Be right back."

Beecher took the elevator, and Grant returned his gaze to the cell monitor recording her every move and word. Madison still stood back to the cameras—but there was a slight movement at her side. Rubbing something inside her pocket… Her medal or his rubbing stone?

Half surprised she hadn't hurled either or both at him, Grant stood up. He couldn't sit here knowing she was hurting and do nothing. He couldn't let them hold her here until she died of old age, either. Snagging a soda from the small fridge tucked under the counter against the back wall, he put in a request for bottled water, then walked the soda down to Madison.

Just outside her cell, he stopped at the bars. "Lunch

is on its way. There wasn't any cold water on hand—I'm getting some brought down—but I brought you a soda."

She glared back at him, her gaze as hard as carved stone.

He passed the can through the bars, mouthed, *I'm going to tell Mrs. Renault. See what she can do.*

Madison took the can, turned her back and whispered, "She knows—and don't you dare make me sorry I trusted you with that."

"Madison, I—I—"

"You what?" The venom in her voice was at total odds with the hurt in her eyes.

Knowing he'd put it there upset Grant more than he could put into words. He had been a warrior, trained to bury his feelings and keep his mouth shut since he'd been an adult. Talking about feelings was hard for him. Almost impossible, but that hadn't been such a bad thing until now. Now, he needed to verbalize for her and for himself, but he couldn't.

No man can serve two masters.

He could honor God by honoring his oath or honor Madison. He couldn't honor both. "I—I'll bring your lunch as soon as it arrives."

"Whatever, Grant. But don't do anything to hurt Mrs. Renault."

"I wouldn't do that."

She looked back at him. "Is that the truth or another of your lies?"

If words could lay a man low, he'd be below the white tile floor. He frowned. "Go ahead and judge me,

Madison. I've earned it." Apparently she needed a little more time to come to terms. He couldn't fault her for questioning his honesty. After all, he'd earned her doubt. In her shoes, he'd be so frosted at what he'd done the cell bars would be dripping icicles.

Done was done, and all he could do now was forge ahead. The question in his mind was two-part. What did Mrs. Renault know about Madison's detainment, and what had she done about it?

Talbot putting her in an adjoining cell wouldn't do a thing for her or to help Madison. And that Mrs. Renault had once been the wife of the Nest commander wouldn't be enough to spare her.

Both women could be in even greater jeopardy. What could Grant do? Could anyone get them through this intact?

He seriously doubted it.

And that worried him most of all.

Three days later, Madison struggled to hold on to hope. Sitting on the floor in the center of her cell, she finished her prayers, and confident the flashbacks haunting her would abate, she opened her eyes.

Grant stood just outside her cell.

"What do you want?" She tried to keep the bite out of her tone. During her time here, he'd tried reassuring her not with words but with actions that he was doing all he could do. Beecher had been distant and withdrawn, but there when needed. It was clear: any help for her would come from Grant.

He beckoned to her, and hesitantly she approached the bars.

"Do you need anything?" Hiding his actions with his body, he passed her a scrap of paper.

She slid it into her pocket. "Other than to get out of here? No." She showed him her medal. "You see this?" Holding it up so the camera would record it, she looked at the medal. "I'm an honored veteran. You're holding me here as if I were a criminal. Someone will have to answer for this, Grant Deaver. Do you hear me? I'm not going to disappear. I have family and friends who won't rest until they find me."

"The odds of that are none," he said softly. "Accept it, and you'll make peace with a lot less agony."

She glared at him. "I'll never accept it."

"Be careful, saying things like that. It narrows their choices, and makes your future more bleak."

He was right about that. She despised it, but facts were facts.

"Did you look at your Purple Heart?" he whispered, his back to the cameras, his voice barely audible.

She cut her eyes left, telling him no, she hadn't.

"Look."

She turned her back, whispered, "Where's Mrs. Renault?"

"Underground. I can't reach her."

Madison looked back at him. Fear flashed in her eyes. "Maggie?"

Her best friend, Maggie Mason, a profiler for the FBI and landscape artist. He shook his head.

"Find her, Grant. Please."

"Trying."

She turned away. "Are you? Really?"

Catching her glance, he let her see the truth in his eyes. *I promise.*

She believed him. Whether or not she should, she couldn't tell, but she did. *Trust your instincts.* She whispered, soft and low. "Try harder."

He blinked once. *Yes.*

"Read, then destroy the note."

She blinked once.

He stepped back. "What day is it?" she asked.

"Monday."

"Night or day?"

Guilt covered him like a coat. "Monday night," he said, then glanced at his watch. "Seven o'clock." He unstrapped the band, stepped close to the bars and passed her his watch. *Who is Janet Hardy?*

Madison searched her mind, mentally reviewed her files. "Never heard of her. Why?"

"Later."

She took the watch and then hid it in her pocket. "Thank you."

"Read the note—and trust me."

Did she dare? Did she? She couldn't say. Maybe after she looked at her Purple Heart and read the note.

He didn't wait for a response, just headed up the center aisle until he disappeared from her sight.

Madison waited an hour before easing the note and her medal out of her pocket. Her thoughts ran wild.

They had been wild since her detention, but Mrs. Renault out of touch for three days? That had to be Talbot. There was no other explanation. The man was in love with her and had been since her husband's death—maybe before, but if so he'd kept his feelings to himself. Which would prove stronger for him? His love for her or his loyalty to his nation? Could he find a way to reconcile both?

She and Grant hadn't, but then Grant hadn't been in love, just doing his job and getting sucked into it personally a little too deep. Deep enough to help her maybe, but not deep enough to love her. And boy, did knowing that hurt.

Disheartened, she sat on the floor, facing the cot and short brick wall that afforded her bathroom privacy, her back to the cameras.

She unfolded the scrap of paper—and heard raised voices coming from the end of the hall. Startled, she crammed the paper and medal back into her pocket and strained to hear what had caused the ruckus.

FIVE

"I can't let you go down there, sir."

Grant squared off at the vice commander. Beecher kept his seat at the observation desk, watching closely but not getting involved.

"Get out of my way, Deaver." Dayton's face flushed red, and the veins in his neck bulged.

"I can't do that, sir. I'm under direct orders from Commander Talbot."

Surprise flitted across Dayton's face. "Why?"

"You'll have to ask him, sir." Grant had been given orders and he hoped to goodness Beecher had, too.

"Is that a fact?" Dayton looked at Beecher.

"Yes, sir." Beecher stood up, moved to Grant's side.

"Fine." He turned on his heel, strode the short distance to the elevator and nearly put his fist through the wall punching the call button.

Grant looked at Beecher, who nodded.

Neither said a thing, but words weren't needed, and for the first time since Talbot had summoned Grant to his office and told him Madison had been detained,

Grant was more worried about what Dayton would do than Talbot.

Beecher passed Grant the red phone. It was a hotline directly to the commander. "Better let him know Dayton's coming."

Grant nodded, sure as certain Talbot had been expecting this call for three days.

Talbot answered. "Yes."

"Vice Commander Dayton just tried to get in to see Madison. We didn't let him. He wasn't happy, sir."

"Is he on his way here?"

"He didn't say, but he was plenty ticked when he left, sir. I'd be expecting him."

"Thanks for the notice."

"Yes, sir."

"Grant, wait."

He put the phone back to his ear. "Yes, sir?"

"Did you give Madison the note?"

His throat went thick. "Yes, sir, I did. Right before Dayton came down."

"So she did read it?"

"I can't say for sure. I heard the elevator chime, so I headed back to the observation desk."

"You've got her on monitors. Ask Beecher."

Grant turned to him. "Did you see her read the note?"

"Her back's been to us the entire time, but I suspect she did."

"Apparently read, sir," Grant said into the phone.

"Good."

The line went dead.

Grant hung up the phone.

"Hate it for you, Grant," Beecher said.

"Yeah." The situation kept getting worse and worse. "Me, too."

Madison read the note on the scrap of paper. *Midnight tonight. Use worry stone to break lightbulb. Vent. Right. Up two. South. Wait for guard change. Woods. Run. Don't come back. 99% sure they've got RR. Trust me.*

RR? *Renée Renault.* A streak of pure fear shot through Madison's body.

She read the note again, committed it to memory and then ate it. So Mrs. Renault had confronted Talbot about Madison. Otherwise he wouldn't have detained her. How could Madison go and sacrifice Mrs. Renault? Did Grant have a plan to get her out, too? Talbot wouldn't hold her at the Nest, not with her history here. These troops respected and loved Mrs. Renault because she loved them. Someone would help her.

Hadn't Mrs. Renault nurtured Madison and agreed to work for her because Madison's vision for Lost, Inc., would help her military family? She didn't have to work; she'd chosen to guide and support and help Madison fulfill her vision, and Madison would never abandon her—and Talbot would know that. Just as Grant knew that confined to this cell, Madison wasn't in a position to help either of them. She had to get out to do either of them any good. He'd told her repeatedly he'd been trying to locate Mrs. Renault. His worry had seemed genuine. But Madison knew better than to trust appearances with him. He was an accomplished deceiver. That she knew for fact.

Was this note a setup? An attempt to get her to escape so they could shoot her? Was that the plan? Or was Grant genuinely fearful for her and Mrs. Renault and trying to help them? And who was this Janet Hardy he'd asked her about? How did she fit in? Madison had never even heard of the woman.

She squeezed her eyes shut. *Oh, I wish I knew what to do.*

Seeking comfort, she pulled her Purple Heart out of her pocket. The pink stone came with it. She pushed it under the edge of her slacks at her thigh. The fabric buried it. Then she rubbed the medal. What should have been smooth felt rough. Something had scratched it.

She lifted it in front of her body, careful to keep it out of the camera's line of sight. The medal was indeed scratched, but it hadn't been an accident.

A thin mark defaced it. A tiny heart.

Grant had lied, but his feelings for her were genuine.

She looked back at the bare lightbulb. *Use worry stone to break lightbulb.*

Under the edge of her slacks, she glimpsed his pink rubbing stone. *Trust.* He'd told her to keep it—and now she knew why.

It and the medal gave her two opportunities to hit the bulb.

Doubt crept in. What if this was a trap? It could be.

Torn and confused on what to do, she tried to sort through and see the situation objectively, see paths to resolutions that left her and Mrs. Renault intact. *There is no way.*

A verse from Isaiah drifted through her mind. *I will go before thee, and make the crooked places straight: I will break in pieces the gates of brass, and cut in sunder the bars of iron...*

She repeated it inside her head over and again, just as she had when detained in Afghanistan.

Calmer then, she checked Grant's watch—10:45. Torn between staying and going, she didn't know what to do, and she had just over an hour to decide.

Since her return to the States, Madison had talked to God, she had prayed to Him, but she had refused to come to Him on bended knee. It wasn't pride that held her back. It was anger. She'd trusted and needed Him and been faithful to Him, and yet in her darkest hour...

She looked at that tiny heart scratched into her medal, and the truth hit her like a sledge.

She'd survived. Against all odds, she'd escaped and made it home.

During that entire ordeal, all along the way, when she'd hit a brick wall, something had happened. Some unseen door had opened, some stranger had crossed her path and done her a kindness.

He'd been with her the whole time.

Tears pooled in her eyes, blurring her vision, and fell to her cheeks. Why hadn't she seen that? Why hadn't she recognized His intervention?

She knelt and uttered a plea for forgiveness, whispered the praise and gratitude now that she should have then.

At 11:30, Beecher appeared outside her cell.

Emotionally exhausted, Madison lay stretched out atop the scratchy green blanket on her cot. She started to fake being asleep, but something warned her against it, so she looked over at him. “What is it, Major Beecher?”

Did he have news for her? He hadn’t shared much in the past three days, just asked her what she wanted to eat or drink, and once he’d told her that Grant wasn’t on-site. He’d gone to the office for something. She’d taken that as he was out looking for information and, she hoped, for Mrs. Renault.

“He hasn’t found her.”

Madison sat straight up. “He hasn’t found whom?”

“Mrs. Renault.” The skin between Beecher’s wide brows furrowed. Clearly he didn’t like what was going on here, but like Grant, he was powerless to stop it. “He just called. Her home was trashed. No sign of her.”

“Where were Talbot and Dayton when it happened?” Madison asked, daring to frown. “I’d start looking there.”

“Talbot was here, and Lieutenant Blake says Dayton was at Miss Addie’s Café.”

“Did you ask Miss Addie?” Madison asked. Why Beecher was coming to her, she had no idea. If Grant had taken him into his confidence, he would have told her. He hadn't, and that meant she had to be very careful about what she said.

"Not yet." He leaned against the bars. "Just wanted you to know."

"I appreciate it." He'd worked with her several times. When a bomb had been planted in her office, he'd disarmed it. When the same man had planted another bomb at the local church during the children's Christmas program, Beecher had disarmed it, too. He had the courage to put himself on the line. She'd personally seen him do it repeatedly. So what was he doing here? What was the unspoken message he was passing her? Was there one, or was this just an update because he couldn't pretend he didn't know her anymore than she could pretend she didn't know him?

"How can you sleep here with that light in your face all night?"

"I can't tell if it's day or night." Her heartbeat sped up. "It doesn't matter. I can't sleep much, anyway."

He glanced up at the bare bulb, and then back to her. "If you need anything, yell."

"Thank you."

He sent her a long, steady look, then nodded.

Madison lay down and faced the back wall, then checked Grant's watch—11:53. Seven minutes.

Decide, Madison. Stay or go? She stared straight up at the grate, her portal to the duct, fully engaged in internal debate, torn on whom, if anyone, to trust.

At exactly one minute to midnight, her debate on

whether Grant or Beecher were helping her or setting her up took an unexpected twist.

The lightbulb went out.

In the dark, Madison stretched to reach the grate. It wasn't screwed in, just resting inside a metal-channeled frame. Was that a sign for good or ill? Unsure, she hoisted herself up, the sharp-edged rim biting into her hands.

Finally she sat huddled inside the vent and gave herself a moment to let her breathing calm. Her hands were tender, and she'd nicked the left one at the big crease. She wet her fingertip on her tongue, and wiped at it, then headed right down the duct, praying she wasn't making the biggest mistake of her life.

Crawling on her hands and knees, she bumped into something—rope. It hung suspended from above inside the duct. Apparently this was where she was to go up two. She tested it for strength and stepped on something—gloves. Grant had to have done this. Sliding her hands into them, she let her fingers run down the length of rope and hit a looped knot. Excellent. She could hoist herself easily with this.

Ten minutes later she came to a T in the duct—obviously the demarcation of the first level. An alien sound snagged her ear. Not crying exactly, but definitely a woman. Could it be Mrs. Renault?

Knowing she should head on up to assure she didn't miss the changing of the guard, Madison still couldn't do it. If that was Mrs. Renault, she needed to know.

Scooting left on all fours, she moved toward the odd sound.

The duct was tighter here, the air moving through it blessedly cool. For that, Madison gave thanks. Closed in was hard. Closed in and hot would have been impossible for her.

The sound got louder. Keening. She crawled over two grates, and at the third, heard the sound clearly.

She bent low and peered down into a cell that looked identical to the one she'd been held in. A brunette in her late forties paced the cell like a half-mad dog, alternating between demanding she be released and screeching at the top of her lungs.

A man strode down the hall. "Knock it off, Janet. That racket hasn't worked for four months and it's not going to work now."

Madison could see only his shoes, but she thought she recognized his voice. *Blake?*

"Get away from my cell, Blake," the woman he'd called Janet told him.

"Lieutenant Blake," he insisted.

"I will not call you by a name reserved for honorable men."

"Oh, you will," he said. "If you want to eat again."

"Why eat? Just means I'll live longer stuck in here."

Definitely the same Lieutenant Blake who'd brought Madison here. And this woman was Janet. Grant had asked her about a Janet.

"Fine by me." A cold edge rippled through his tone. "Take yourself out. It'll spare us the trouble."

Fading footfalls sounded—Blake walking away.

The woman went silent. She waited a full minute, then looked up at the grate and whispered, "Who are you?"

Madison was stunned.

"I made enough noise to wake the dead to cover for you. The least you can do is tell me who you are."

"Madison McKay."

"I'm Janet Hardy."

"Why are you here?" Madison whispered.

"Sometimes it isn't what you know but who you know."

"I don't follow."

"I had the poor judgment to make some phone call records disappear. Crazy as I surely am, I actually did it, and then it dawned on me what I'd done. I tried to make myself disappear, but I wasn't fast enough. They got me."

Madison's heart skipped a full beat. "The phone call to Brett Lund, the WKME station manager. You wiped out the records of who he talked to right before—"

"He killed himself. Yes. Stupid, I surely am." She let out a disgusted rumble.

"Who made you do it?"

"Got a written order for it. It was signed. I'm sorry to say I didn't think much of it at the time so I just did it, and filed it. Blake—the jerk who just left here—came looking for the order. When I couldn't produce it, he was pretty upset. I guess I misfiled the thing. Anyway, after that little run-in, I knew I was in trouble. So I was preparing to run, only Blake caught me and hauled me in for questioning. I've been stuck here ever since."

Blake worked for Talbot. So he'd been tying up loose ends and couldn't because an order had been misfiled. No doubt he'd torn up every file cabinet in Janet Hardy's office. "Did he find the order?"

"If he had, I figure I'd be dead."

"Was Blake there for Talbot or Dayton?"

"I don't know." She paused, urgency filling her stage whisper. "Someone's coming. Go on and get out of here, but send back help."

Mrs. Renault. "Is anyone else being held here?"

"Not on this cellblock." She hesitated. "Madison, don't forget me."

Hearing the pleading in her voice, Madison promised, "I won't."

Madison began to move. She crawled down the duct back to the up chute, hooked her foot into the looped rope and then began hoisting herself.

At the next landing she removed the gloves and set them on the floor near the rope, then at a grate leaned close to see below and stared right at a stairwell door. To the right, she felt a soft bundle—a military uniform.

It would help her get past any guards, should she encounter them. Hopefully, they could be avoided.

She tugged the pants and shirt on over her clothes and then moved the grate. She couldn't leave it open. In the sterile corridor, not five feet down from the grate, she spotted a chair—obviously Grant had prepositioned it to aid her reach. She snagged it, replaced the grate, then returned the chair to its place and took the stairs up to ground level at a run, her heart pounding hard enough to crack bone.

At the top, the stairwell ended at a door. She scanned for signs of an alarm, but saw none. Holding her breath, prepared for a blast of noise, she turned the knob.

The door swung open and cold air gushed into her face. Fresh air. *Thank You, God.* She looked left then right and saw no one. Stepping away from the building, she craned her neck to look up at the roof. No soldiers. No one standing guard every twenty feet around the building's perimeter or above. *Odd.* But she was on the back side of the building away from the roadways leading to it. Still, there should be guards. Leaving your back open? Not a proven tactical position. Grant must have done something.

Think later. Move now.

She made a beeline for the woods, running full out, and with two steps to go to the cover of safety, a man charged out in front of her. "Grant?"

He snagged her arm, pulled her to him, wrapping her in a fierce hug. "Madison."

He was shaking hard. "What's wrong?"

"You have to go back."

"What?" She pulled away from him.

"I can't explain. But I'm begging you to trust me. You have to go back—now, before anyone finds out you're missing."

Panic flushed through her body. "I can't go back there. You know how hard being confined is—"

"I do know, and I know this could end very badly. But if you don't go back, I know it definitely *will* end badly. This is your one chance, Madison. Please."

"Beecher turned off the lights. Is he working for Blue Shoes?"

"I can't answer that." Grant stroked her face. "Madison, we don't have time. We just don't. You're going to have to trust me."

She stilled, looked up at him. Pale moonlight lit up his face. "I do trust you. I'm out here, aren't I?"

"Yes, you are." He smiled, and touched a grateful kiss to her lips. "You looked at the medal."

"Yes." Madison held a stitch in her side. "Oh, I ran into Janet Hardy."

"You know who she is, then?"

"I do now. She expunged the phone records on Lund under a written order. Lieutenant Blake showed up wanting it. She'd misfiled it and was preparing to run when they hauled her in. She says she's been detained here ever since."

Grant released her. "Beecher told me she was detained—that's why I asked you about her. I didn't know if she was connected to your cases."

"I wasn't holding out on you. I just didn't know who she was until she told me."

"You've got to get back."

She didn't move. "It's clear Lieutenant Blake is working for Blue Shoes. But is Blue Shoes Commander Talbot or Dayton?"

Grant scanned the area. "I'm still vetting them both."

That was honest. She tiptoed, pecked a kiss on his lips. "I'm putting my life—and probably Janet Hardy's—in your hands. Don't make me regret it. And don't linger. I've got to get out of here and find Mrs. Renault." Madison frowned. "Or is she here, too?"

"I've checked every cellblock. She's not here."

"Beecher said her house was trashed."

Grant nodded. "I think that was just noise to cover her disappearance."

"Did you get everyone at the agency on it?"

"No, I said the two of you went on a fact-finding trip."

She stilled. "Why?"

"Don't look at me like that, okay? The more people who know about this, the greater the odds are we'll get neither of you out of here nor any of us out of this alive." He frowned. "Madison, we don't have time for this. You've got to trust me."

The pleading in his voice shot straight to her heart. "I do." Something struck her foot. A stone. She kicked it away and looked back up at him. "If anything happens to me, I want your promise that you'll keep looking for Mrs. Renault until you find her. You'll never give up." Madison's throat went tight. "Promise me?"

He clasped her arms, looked her right in the eye. "I promise." He hugged her quickly, then turned her back toward the building. "Go, and hurry, Madison."

"The chair at the stairs." She shot him a worried look. "I can't put it back and get in through the grate."

"I'll handle the chair. Be right behind you."

She nodded. "Be careful."

"You, too."

Madison ran back toward the building. When she disappeared inside, Grant pulled out his cell phone.

A man answered. "Yes?"

"She's on her way back to her cell."

"Good. We're ready, then."

"We, sir?" What did he mean, *we?*

The line went dead.

The question unanswered, Grant stowed his phone with a heavy heart full of fear, and ran for the building.

Madison dropped down into her cell.

"Thank God."

Scared stiff at hearing another woman's voice, she spun around. "Mrs. Renault?" She stooped, hunched down behind the short brick wall.

"Yes, it's me," she whispered. "Lower your voice."

"How did you get here?"

"Special invitation. It came right after I demanded to know where you were," she whispered.

"Talbot detained you in my cell?"

Metal clanked—a key in the cell door. "Renée? Where are you?"

Talbot! Madison stood between them. "It's Madison, Commander."

"Renée. Now!"

She stood up. "I'm right here, Andrew." She walked around the short wall and stood next to Madison.

"Come with me. Both of you." He opened the door.

Madison moved to leave the cell, and Mrs. Renault shot out an arm, blocking her, squaring off on Talbot. "The spinner spins gold for whom?"

Shock crossed his face. He didn't move, just stared at her a long moment. Mrs. Renault didn't flinch or speak, just held his gaze with her own, uncompromising.

"Rumpelstiltskin," he whispered in a faint voice barely recognizable as belonging to him.

"Let's go," Mrs. Renault told Madison. "Andrew Talbot is innocent. Dayton is Blue Shoes. He killed David Pace and, I strongly suspect, Beth Crane."

"What?" What had just happened here?

"Just move," Mrs. Renault said, leaving the cell, urging Madison with her.

They walked right past the observation desk she'd seen on her way in. Neither Beecher nor Grant was manning it. Talbot reached into the monitor, removed the disc and shoved it into his pocket. "Follow me."

He guided them through a series of tunnels that had more twists and turns than a pretzel. They passed at least a dozen doors, none of which were marked. Only by walking them many times could anyone recall the path.

Finally he pulled out a key and opened a door. "Wait here a second." He stared at Renée. "Do not move."

She nodded.

Less than a minute later, he returned. "Come in."

He'd cleared…his office? He was connected directly to the Nest by a series of underground tunnels.

Talbot closed the door and keyed the lock. "Stay put. Help yourself to whatever you find in the fridge."

"Where are you going, Andrew?" Mrs. Renault followed him to the outer office door.

He paused. "Don't open this door for anyone but me or Grant. Understood?"

Mrs. Renault nodded, and asked her question a second time. "Where are you going?"

Talbot sent her a level look. "To see if Dayton took the bait."

Madison lifted a hand. "Watch out for Lieutenant Blake. He's working with him."

"Actually, he's not."

"Sir, I beg to differ." Madison hiked her chin. "Janet Hardy would, too."

He paused. Both he and Mrs. Renault looked at Madison as if she'd sprouted two heads. "What do you know about Janet Hardy?" Mrs. Renault asked.

"I know she's been in a cell here for four months. Ever since Lieutenant Blake brought her here because she couldn't produce the written order to expunge the phone records."

"Which phone records?" Talbot asked, clearly disturbed to learn Lieutenant Blake was playing both sides of the fence.

"Oh, good grief." Mrs. Renault motioned with her hand. "The call to the WKME station manager, Brett Lund. Right after his discussion with Ian and Maggie about his reporters, David Pace and Beth Crane, on the Nest, Lund took the call and then shot himself, remember?"

"I remember."

She sat down in his desk chair. "Ah, of course." Something had become clear to her. "The call was made from the installation, so it had to go. Crawford couldn't be blamed for that one. He must have had an airtight alibi for that time." She swiveled to look at Madison. "Was Dayton the caller?"

"I don't know. Janet Hardy might. She couldn't remember who had signed the expunge order—"

"Only two people could," Talbot said. "Dayton or me, and I didn't, so he must have."

Madison nodded. "She might remember the number, considering it's changed her whole life."

"Where is she?" Talbot asked.

Madison told him.

He grabbed the doorknob. "Do not leave this office and remember, no one comes in but Grant or me."

"We'll remember." Mrs. Renault stood up. "Do be careful, Andrew."

He nodded, the look in his eyes warming, then left and locked the door.

Madison walked to the fridge and got a soda. "Want one?"

"Yes, please."

She passed one of the cans to Mrs. Renault, then opened her own. It fizzed. After taking a drink, she asked the question most pressing in her mind. "You want to explain that gold spinner, Rumpelstiltskin thing to me?"

She gave Madison an enigmatic smile. "Something I picked up from my late husband."

Madison sat down in the visitor's chair and waited.

Mrs. Renault dropped her voice. "It's a question that shouldn't have to be asked but…" The corners of her mouth drew down. "Andrew Talbot isn't the first commander to have a vice commander he isn't sure he can trust."

Madison processed that. "So if asked the question, the commander has two possible answers," Madison guessed. "If he trusts him, he gives one, and—"

"If not, he gives the other," Mrs. Renault said. "Andrew does not trust Jeremy Dayton."

That Mrs. Renault knew the question and the answer, and what it meant, explained the surprised look on Talbot's face. "He wasn't aware you knew that," Madison said. "I'm surprised he responded."

"He trusts me, and I trust him." She sipped from her soda. "I also have all the clearances required to ask. For me, it was a safety issue. It's different for the commanders, of course."

A secret signal. "I see." Madison hadn't realized that commanders' spouses were in such positions, though on thinking about it, she should have realized it. They were rich targets.

"I've suspected him for some time," Mrs. Renault admitted.

"Since when?" Why hadn't she said something?

"Remember before Christmas when Maggie Mason fled Illinois and Andrew brought her back from Nashville on his plane?"

Her best friend, Maggie, had been trying to outrun a serial killer. Madison remembered it all too well.

"During that debacle, she said she'd seen a pair of neon-blue aquatic shoes in either Talbot's or Dayton's suitcase. Remember that?"

Madison did remember them discussing it in a phone conference with all the staff. "She wasn't sure whose case it was."

"I was nearly sure," Mrs. Renault said. "It's rare for a commander to drag his own bag. Typically, someone carries it for him."

Whether or not there was validity in that observation, Mrs. Renault would know better than Madison. But it seemed plausible. "So why didn't you mention it?"

"I did," she said. "Just not to you. I mentioned it to Andrew."

"So he knew Dayton was Blue Shoes all this time and he said nothing?"

"He didn't know it any more than I knew it. He suspected. He's been trying to gather evidence. You don't ruin a man's career or doubt his service to his country without indisputable proof, Madison. Once drawn into doubt, he can never recover. That's why it was imperative that this be done very discreetly and with as few people aware as possible." She propped an arm on his desk and tapped her fingertips against her cheek. "I expect he would have had the proof if Blake hadn't been double-crossing him."

"Yeah, nothing can wreck a good investigation quicker than a mole batting for the other side."

Her expression hardened. "He'll regret that."

Madison was sure he would.

Someone knocked on the door. Mrs. Renault pressed a shushing fingertip against her lips.

"It's Andrew, Renée. Let me in."

She opened the door and Andrew all but shoved Janet Hardy into the office. "Keep her here until I get back."

"Where's Grant?"

"If he's where he should be, down in your cell." Talbot shut the door and Mrs. Renault locked it.

Fear punched the breath out of Madison. "Grant is the bait!"

SIX

"Why is it so dark down that corridor, Beecher?"

Beecher's voice carried to Grant down the cellblock's center isle. "Bulb burned out, sir. Maintenance put me on a list. There aren't any spares on hand down here."

Dayton nodded. "Is she giving you any trouble?"

"No, sir. The light has been keeping her awake. Since it blew, she's been sleeping like a rock."

The desk phone rang. Beecher answered it. "Cell-block D., Major Beecher." A pause, then Beecher told Dayton, "Sir, it's Lieutenant Blake."

"Tell him I'll call him back."

Grant lay on Madison's cot and pulled the covers up, then half covered his head with a pillow. The spill-over light was dim but if Dayton caught so much as a glimpse of Grant's brown hair rather than Madison's silver-blond, he'd probably shoot first and ask questions later. Where was the commander? He should have been here before now.

"McKay?" Dayton raised his voice outside the bars. "Get up."

Grant didn't move.

"McKay." He mumbled something about all the trouble she'd been. "On your feet."

Grant still didn't move. He hoped that Beecher called to see what the holdup was with Talbot—and that the man arrived before Dayton put a bullet in him.

Keys rattled. Dayton was unlocking the cell, and he'd pulled his weapon.

The jig was up.

And the last remnants of doubt fled. Dayton had not come to talk to Madison. He'd come to kill her.

The red phone rang.

Madison held out a staying hand. "Don't answer—"

Mrs. Renault lifted the receiver. "Commander Talbot's office. May I ask who's calling?"

"It's Beecher," the man whispered. "Dayton's at Madison's cell. There was no stopping him from going down there. I warned him again that we were under direct orders, but short of shooting him, I couldn't stop him."

"Thank you." She dropped the receiver. "Something's happened to Andrew," she told Madison, her calm exterior cracking. "Let's go."

"Who was that?" Madison asked, one hand on the doorknob.

"Beecher. Dayton's at your cell."

"It's empty." So what was making Mrs. Renault worry?

"It's not," she said. "I think Grant is in it."

The bait! Madison took off running. Mrs. Renault and Janet Hardy followed her. *Oh, please let him be okay. Please, don't let him be hurt, protecting me. Please!*

"Andrew's not there." Mrs. Renault paused, swiped off her heels and ran faster. "You know he should be. Beecher calling is a bad, bad sign."

Madison had to agree, but held off saying so. They took the shortest path down to the cellblock. "Elevator," Madison said, pointing to the half-open door.

On the floor inside it lay Andrew Talbot.

Janet Hardy gasped. "Is he dead?"

Renée dropped to her knees, checked his carotid. The relief that swept over her face said all that needed saying. He was alive.

"Andrew. Andrew." She dragged her fingertips down his face.

"Renée." He let out a contented sigh.

"Andrew." She lightly slapped him. "Come out of it."

His eyes sprang open. "I told you not to leave my—"

"Where's Grant?" Madison cut in.

"In your cell. We pulled a sting on Dayton."

She reached to his waist and snatched his gun. "Is he armed?"

"Grant?"

"Dayton." Madison resisted grinding her teeth.

"Always." Talbot grabbed his head. "Renée, I think I'm going to be sick."

"It'll be okay, dear." She ran her fingertips along his scalp, checking for wounds. "You've taken a healthy rap to the head." She looked back. "Go, Madison. Janet, get that trash can, will you?" She pointed her chin. "There, by the vending machine."

Janet rushed to get the can.

Madison left them in the hall.

"She can't face Dayton alone." Janet shoved the can at him, and he retched.

"Better now?" Renée asked.

He nodded, hauled himself to his feet. "Let's go." Talbot swayed. "Dayton will do his best to kill them both."

"Madison?" Beecher's mouth dropped open.

She lifted a shushing finger to her mouth. "Dayton is Blue Shoes."

Beecher jumped to his feet and pulled his gun. "You're sure?"

"Positive." She nodded down the center corridor. "Is he down at my cell?"

Beecher nodded. "I thought you were in it asleep."

She shook her head. "It's Grant."

"Hang back. I'll take the lead."

Madison was out front and off down the corridor before he fully finished the sentence. Dayton wasn't in the corridor. He had to be inside the cell with Grant. Fearing what that could mean, she clung to the side of the corridor, the metal bars brushing against her back, giving her maximum potential for getting close without being seen.

Beecher followed, his breaths sweeping over her right shoulder.

Voices carried down the hallway.

"Deaver?" Dayton sounded surprised. "What are you doing here? Did Madison give you the slip?"

Grant answered, "She's with the commander."

"Where did he take her?"

"I don't know, sir. He didn't say."

A pause. Madison used it to step out and look into the cell. Dayton was holstering his gun. She motioned for Beecher to stay put.

"Hands up, Dayton." She trained the commander's weapon on him.

He reached for his gun. Grant blocked him. They scuffled in the deep shadows. Beecher rounded her and burst into the cell, letting out a growl that had the hair on Madison's neck standing on end.

Bone cracked. "Grant, enough." She rushed into the cell. "Enough!"

He grabbed Dayton's gun and patted him down, then snagged an arm. Beecher latched on to the other.

"Let go of me, Major. That's a direct order."

"Sorry, Blue Shoes," Grant said. "We don't take orders from killers, and you're under arrest."

"Have you lost your mind?"

"Trusting you? Probably." Beecher began reading him his rights.

The commander, Mrs. Renault and Janet Hardy hurried toward the cell and paused outside it. Lieutenant

Blake came up behind them, and he seemed rattled, his eyes darting, his face splotched red.

So the commander was going to let Blake hang himself with his own rope, Madison surmised. Fine, so long as he did it. Janet Hardy hung back, planting herself between Blake and any escape route.

Talbot looked at Grant. “Lock Dayton in Madison’s cell.”

“You’d better put her in it,” Dayton said. “Or when I get through talking, you’ll both be in one.”

“No, we won’t,” Talbot said. “We’ve suspected you were Blue Shoes for some time. Mrs. Renault and Madison have been working with me to flush you out, and now we have.”

“No one will believe that.”

“We have the evidence to prove it,” Talbot said. “Mrs. Renault has been in constant touch on behalf of Lost, Inc.” He nodded at Grant. “Lock him up.”

Grant and Beecher stepped out of the cell and Grant swung the door shut, then locked it.

The click reverberated down the corridor.

Grant stepped to her side and Madison reminded him, “The vent.”

“Handled it.”

“Finally got him, sir.” Blake smiled at the commander.

“Finally got you both, Lieutenant.” Talbot nodded to Beecher. “Lock Blake up, too.”

“Sir?” Blake looked stunned but it wasn’t faked. It

showed in every expression flitting over his face. "I've worked this with you all the way."

"And you've worked it with Dayton. No matter who won or lost, you were set, right, Blake?" Talbot's face went from stern to grim. "Get him out of my sight."

Beecher walked him down to the other end of the cellblock and locked him inside, then read him his rights through the bars.

"I want a lawyer."

"You waived rights to counsel when you signed on at the Nest," Madison reminded him. "We all did."

Mrs. Renault stepped closer to Andrew. "We should have someone look at your head. You've got a goose egg. Dayton knocked you out, right?"

"Caught me in the elevator." He nodded. "Can you drive me over to the hospital?"

"Of course." She looked at the others. "Janet, stay put with Major Beecher until we get back. Andrew is going to want to talk with you to make sure you get all you need before returning home—provided that's the safest place for you."

"Yes, ma'am." Her expression darkened. "I'm not going back into that cell."

"Of course not."

Madison recalled her escape in Afghanistan. She'd yearned for a shower and clean clothes, a decent meal and fresh air. Janet had been spared from those kinds of things. Her hair smelled of shampoo, her clothes were crisp and clean and the scent of soap clung to her skin. She hadn't been a prisoner, though she'd been detained.

While challenges lay ahead, they wouldn't include the aftereffects of being deprived of necessities.

Beecher escorted Janet to the observation desk. "Can I buy you a soft drink?"

She smiled, and her eyes lit up. "Thank you."

"Can you call in backup to help you here?" Grant asked Beecher.

"Yeah, I'll get some of my team in. They never liked Dayton. They'll fight for the honor of the extra duty."

Grant smiled. "I'm going to get Madison home, then I'll be back."

Beecher nodded and turned back to Janet Hardy.

Madison couldn't wait to get outside.

The first crisp breath made her heady. So heady she forgot herself and locked Grant in a fierce hug.

Surprised, he wrapped his arms around her and held her close. "You okay?"

"I'm on the back side of being scared to death." She buried her face in his neck. "Finding out you'd set yourself up as bait for me, then finding Talbot coldcocked in the elevator and seeing Dayton aiming his weapon at you… I don't ever want to be that afraid again, Grant Deaver."

Fear for him. She more than cared. To react like this, she had to more than care. Grant stroked her jaw tenderly. "I'm fine."

"I know that now. But it terrified me, Grant. Dayton could have shot you." She burrowed closer, held him tighter.

He could barely draw breath…but if he had to give up breathing to keep her in his arms, open and drawing him into her tight inner circle to tell him what she was really thinking and feeling, then he'd gladly do it. This was trust. Showing him her vulnerability, letting him see her fear. A rare thing, definitely, and a privilege hard won.

A sergeant and a captain walked past them in the parking lot and saluted. His arms still wrapped around Madison, Grant lifted one to return their salutes.

All three men smiled, and Madison surely saw it. Knowing it was at her expense, she didn't let him go. "You okay now?" Grant dropped a kiss to her head, and then added, "We should go."

"In a minute. I'm not done yet."

Frankly, neither was he. The adrenaline surge hadn't worn down, and the relief that Blue Shoes was finally behind bars and she was safe was still settling in for them both.

And so they stood another long minute, letting the tension subside, secure in the knowledge that their relationship had finally found a firm footing in trust.

Later, in the kitchen at Lost, Inc., Madison sat beside Grant and glanced out the window. Not quite dawn, the sky was just starting to lighten, strands of pink and gold barely showing on the horizon. The office was silent, except for the drip of the coffeemaker. No one else had arrived yet for the workday and, grateful for the respite, Madison watched Grant rise, fill their favorite mugs with steaming hot coffee, then carry them back to the table.

He slid her Minnie Mouse mug to her. "There you go."

"Thanks."

"Mmm." He swallowed a deep sip. "Are you up for a deep and serious talk?"

"Honestly, I'm not." She took a sip. The heat felt good on her parched throat. "I'm eager for answers, but they can wait." She turned toward him and wrapped her arms around his neck. "This can't." She kissed him fully, completely, openly, holding nothing back. All her fear for him and of him, her worry about the situation, even her upset over the case, swirled and drained under the tenderness of his mouth on hers.

Grant finally broke their kiss and looked into her eyes. "I know you still expect full answers and explanations on everything."

She nodded.

"And I expect you'll scream at me until my ears bleed for doing what I did."

"I have to tell you, I'm so relieved you're alive and Dayton didn't shoot you that you might just get off easier—not a lot, but a little."

He brushed back a strand of her hair. "Grace and mercy are welcome traits."

Emotion swelled in her chest, making it tight. She curled her hand at his jaw, not surprised it was trembling. "Thank you for not dying on me, Grant."

"Likewise, Madison."

Looking into his eyes, she blinked hard and fast. "I—I can't imagine me without you. Not anymore."

He didn't smile. But the twinkle burned bright in his eyes. "God's been good to me, and I have so much to be thankful for, but I'm most thankful you're in my life. I didn't want to lose you, Madison. I didn't see how I couldn't, but—"

She let out a delicate grunt. "We'll see what you think about that after we talk about all this. You might have a few things challenge the top spot on your thankful list."

"Oh, I hope not. I've had enough challenges lately. I could use a break."

She gave him a Mona Lisa smile. "We'll see about that, too."

Grant couldn't take it anymore.

It'd been three days since he had walked out of the Nest with Madison and still she remained not ready to hear what he had to say about anything.

She kissed him. Hugged him. Was nice to him. Ate meals with him. Laughed with him. But she wouldn't let him talk about anything except the mundane and insignificant.

Why? What was she doing?

In addition to making him crazy, that was.

Clearly, he had to do something, but what, he had no idea. He needed help. And only one person in the world might have the insight he lacked and be able to help him.

He walked down the Lost, Inc., hallway, and knocked on the door of the one woman in the world who possibly understood Madison. "Mrs. Renault?" He paused at her open door. It always smelled so good in her office. Fresh flowers. She brought them in every day. "Do you have a minute?"

"Of course, Grant." She closed a file on her desk and slid it aside. "What can I do for you?"

Now that he was here, he wasn't certain how to bring up the subject, or even certain he should. "How's the commander's head?"

"He still has a nasty headache, but he's been back for a follow-up visit with his doctor, and he says he's fine. If he had been hit another inch closer to the temple, we'd be wearing black. Stunning how fragile we are for all our strength, isn't it?"

"Yes, it is. I'm glad he's doing well." Still mentally stumbling in a tug-of-war on whether or not to discuss Madison, Grant just stood here. He should leave, but if he didn't talk to her, he'd stay trapped in this maze until who knew when.

"Anything else I can do for you?"

"I'm floundering," he admitted, letting her see his anguish.

Her expression softened. Encouraged, he pressed on. "She won't talk to me. I mean, we talk, but we don't really talk—about anything that matters." He paced in front of her fireplace. "I keep trying to explain myself, but she cuts me off. She just won't listen." He stopped suddenly and dragged an agitated hand through his hair.

"At the rate we're going, we'll die of old age before I can even ask for her forgiveness much less get her interested in the real me."

Mrs. Renault, who took serious exception to touching her own face in public, covered her mouth with her hand.

"Are you laughing at me?" He was spilling his guts and she was laughing? "You find this amusing?"

"Absolutely not. I'm not laughing—I'm shocked."

"Oh." About what? Him? Madison? Them? What?

"And relieved." She lifted her shoulders. "I've been doubtful she would ever let anyone close to her, and now she has."

"Maybe we've got a communications break here. She won't talk to me or hear me out. She's pushing me away."

"Oh, quite the opposite, Grant." A little bemused, Mrs. Renault curled her fingers to her jaw and looked over at him. "Remember, my dear, our Madison was confined. Think about what that did to her. Think about the joy that comes after it, at being free." Mrs. Renault removed her glasses from her nose. "Right now, Madison is giving birth to her future. She's looking ahead from a joyful place."

"How is her not hearing me out a joyful place?"

"After being confined in Afghanistan, she didn't have the opportunity to embrace that joyful place. All of her energy and thoughts were laser-focused on getting out of that country and back here. When she did, she still was denied joy. Her parents were shadows of their former selves. They'd grieved so hard for her, shells of them were all that was left. She couldn't rejoice then."

"No," he said, sitting down in her visitor's chair and bracing his arms on his knees. "That had to devastate her all over again."

"It did," Mrs. Renault said, sadness in her eyes and her tone. "She had to devote herself to restoring them, and by the grace of God and with His help, she did."

Grant followed her train of thought. "But even then, she couldn't be joyful. She had to make sure it didn't happen to someone else."

"Yes." Mrs. Renault sighed. "Building Lost, Inc., from the ground up, hiring other wounded souls to help her. Still, she had no time to indulge in the gift of just being free to do as she pleased—not while lost ones awaited rescue."

Grant's heart felt squeezed at the urgency driving Madison. Year after year, always putting others and their needs first. "But there'll always be someone lost waiting, Mrs. Renault."

"Yes, there will." Sadness filled her eyes. "That she can't rescue them all is the demon that torments Madison. It isn't that she doesn't know that she can't save them all. It's that she refuses to accept it."

Grant let that roll over in his mind. "She's following her purpose."

"Yes." Mrs. Renault seemed pleased that he'd gotten it. Grant recalled the many hours he'd agonized at trying to do his duty, keep his promises and oaths and not betray Madison. Being at odds and torn between the three was an emotional tightrope that kept him torn up inside and struggling for balance.

"I'm well aware you understand these things. You've had your own purpose to follow, and it's been difficult at times."

"Yes."

"Madison is determined to do everything humanly possible to help them all, even at her own expense. And with her trust issue… Of course, she's worked through that, at least with a few of us."

Did she still trust him? She said she did, but when things settled down, would she? Grant frowned. "The risks that she takes worry me."

"I can see that."

He laced his hands. "Mrs. Renault, it's been my experience that when you give everything, you lose something. If Madison doesn't accept that she can't save all the lost—"

"She'll lose herself." Mrs. Renault nodded. "Which is why I'm here. To help make sure that doesn't happen."

"She's lucky to have you."

She gave him the infamous brow lift. "When Madison came home, I realized quickly I had to do more than worry about her." She tilted her head. "We all have our purpose."

"You admire her."

"Enormously."

"She loves you."

"It's mutual. She's the daughter of my heart, Grant."

Realization dawned. Being a commander's wife most of her adult life, Mrs. Renault had a deep admiration and genuine affection for those who served, and fierce protective instincts. Aligning with Madison had been to help Madison. But Mrs. Renault was every bit as determined to save the lost as her boss.

"So you see, until this moment, Madison has been out of balance, so to speak. Single-mindedly focused on fulfilling her purpose but burying herself and her needs. God wants us to be joyful, and she's finally recognizing that and giving joy its proper place in her life." Mrs. Renault's lips curved in a soft smile. "You're afraid she hates you, but she doesn't, my dear. In her way, she's celebrating her life, and you're a big part of that."

"So I shouldn't push her to let me explain."

"She's waited a long time to feel joyful, Grant. Why not give her a little time to get used to it." She sniffed. "I imagine she's groping to come to terms with it, and it hasn't yet settled in."

He understood all this but remained a little confused. "I totally get her joy at being free. I don't get the way she's treating me."

"How is she treating you?"

"Well, she's not tense or wary. She's being...well, wonderful." He frowned at Mrs. Renault. "You know that's just not normal Madison behavior—not with me. I understood her when she suspected I was spying on her and her staff. I went through the same counterintelligence training she did. Her behavior made sense. But I violated her trust and that was a huge issue with her before then. Trusting me at all was really hard for her, but she did it, and yet learning I crossed her doesn't seem to have impacted her. I don't understand that. You say she doesn't hate me, but I wonder if she really does. Or maybe she's setting me up as payback."

"How uncharacteristically cynical, even for you, Grant. Rethink your conclusions, dear."

He'd missed the mark. Everything in Mrs. Renault's reaction proved it. He stared out the window and watched cars go down the street, even more confused than when he'd entered her office.

"Doubt is a mean taskmaster," she said. "It'll lay claim wherever it finds a welcome sign, earned or not. Madison cares for you. When she discovered the truth, she had to make a choice. The easy, obvious one. Or the more difficult one."

"I wish she'd just yell at me and get it over with—once and for... That's why she's doing it."

"That would ease your conscience, wouldn't it? Make you feel better about your own actions."

It would, but Madison wasn't trying to ease his conscience. She wanted him to stew in guilt. Thunder crossed his expression. "Thanks, Mrs. Renault. Finally this is making sense." He stormed out of her office.

Mrs. Renault rolled her gaze. She'd tried to tell him, but he'd heard only what he'd been ready, willing and able to hear. This was Madison joyful. She wasn't plotting his misery. She was healing.

Mrs. Renault reached for the file she'd been working on before his interruption.

Sooner or later, he'd figure it out.

Madison sat in her office, leaning back with her bare feet propped on her desk, reviewing her lead investigator Della Jackson's new case-status report. She was getting better at meeting her deadlines—this report was only a week late—but considering she'd just returned from her honeymoon with her new husband, Paul Mason, and she was helping her new sister-in-law, Madison's best friend, Maggie Mason, plan her wedding, Madison was just fine with Della's report being tardy. Seeing them all so happy was worth a week. Two weeks, even.

Grant stormed in. "Madison, we need to talk."

She lowered her legs and slid on her flats. "What's wrong?" She set the file down on her desk. "You look—"

"I want to clear the air between us, and I want to do it now." He sat down on the corner of her desk, crowding her knees. "I don't know if you're playing some game with me or what you're thinking about us, and frankly it's making me crazy."

"What?" He thought he was clueless? She wasn't feeling very connected herself at the moment. "I have no idea what you're talking about, Grant." Her stomach sank. "I thought things were going well with us."

So this was the tack he was going to take. He couldn't bring himself to betray her and then just walk out of her life as if it all had meant nothing, so he staged this big breakup scene to soothe his conscience. The bright and shiny and new had worn off, and it had taken only three days. Her heart shattered. So much for believing it was possible he really did care for her.

"Things are going great—and that's the problem." He glared at her. "Four months we've been together and not a day—not one—has been smooth sailing, Madison." He lifted a hand toward her. "This woman isn't you. I don't know what kind of game you're playing, but I don't like it. I'm trying over and over to explain why I did what I did, and you won't let me say a word about it. I can't talk, much less get you to listen to me."

Furious, she stood up. "I'm not playing anything." She curled her hands at her sides. "I've walked in your world. I know why you did what you did. I've been showing you that no explanation is required because—" she raised her voice "—I trust you."

"You trust me." He let out a sigh that would power a wind farm for a month.

"Unconditionally!" She glared back at him. "Though at the moment, I'm having a hard time—"

The phone rang.

She snatched it up. "Yes."

"Andrew phoned," Mrs. Renault said. "I realize you and Grant are, um, in conference, but Andrew says it's vital he speak to you both now. He wants you to come to his office right away."

"Thank you." Madison hung up the phone and met

Grant's gaze. "Command performance in Talbot's office."

"About what?"

"I don't know, but he wants us there now and he says it's vital." She opened a desk drawer and retrieved her purse.

"Madison, wait." Grant touched her shoulder. "I—I—"

She covered his hand with hers. "I know, Grant. Me, too."

"No, this time I will say what I intend to say."

She tensed, waited. *Please, don't let it be something awful.*

His expression turned tender. "I care about you."

Madison smiled. "I care about you, too." She raised a hand to cup his jaw. "Are you worried?"

"About Talbot? Yes." Grant frowned. "So much has happened and I thought things were going to settle down—"

"I meant, are you worried about us?"

He hesitated, then spilled out the truth. "Absolutely."

"Have a little faith." She repeated to him the same thing she'd been telling herself for the past three days. "Things will work out exactly as they're supposed to work out."

"Will that be with us being together?"

She headed toward the door. "I don't know." Didn't she wish she did! "That's where the faith comes in."

"Madison—"

"We need to go now, Grant," she interrupted. "Talbot's waiting."

SEVEN

With Lieutenant Blake no longer manning the gate to Talbot's office, Madison wasn't surprised to see Beecher sitting at that outer desk.

"Been demoted?" Grant asked, a teasing lilt in his tone.

Beecher nodded. "Until this thing with Dayton and Blake is settled, it appears so. But I'm looking at it as a lateral move."

Madison couldn't resist piping in to defend Talbot's choice. "He needs people he can trust close to him."

"You'll move up the ranks, Beecher. He'll see to it," Grant said.

"Not complaining." Worry flooded his eyes. "Just hoping when all the dust settles, he's still standing."

"What's going on?" Grant asked.

"It's best if he explains." He lifted the phone. "They're here, sir," he said into the receiver.

Beecher was more than a little concerned, and for far more than just his own career. That didn't bode well, and from Grant's suddenly grim expression, he, too, knew it.

The heavy metal door into Talbot's office opened and he appeared at it. "Grant. Madison. Thanks so much for coming." Talbot ushered them into his office, shut the door behind them and then motioned to the visitor's chairs. "Sit down."

"You said it was vital we get here right away." Madison took the seat on the right. The leather seemed to melt under her, soft as butter.

When Grant took the seat beside her, Talbot rounded his desk and sat down in his desk chair. Its springs creaked under his weight.

"It is. I've got a dilemma," Talbot said. "After all that's happened, I have no right to ask for your help, but I am. This is bigger than me and, frankly, bigger than the two of you. It's a matter of national security."

Madison eased her hand in her pocket and rubbed her medal. It clacked against Grant's pink rubbing stone. "Commander, why don't you just share what's wrong? Obviously, whatever we can do, we'll do."

Grant nodded, affirming his stance.

"Thank you. Under the circumstances, that's gracious of you both."

Gracious? Grant was active duty. He was compelled. Madison wasn't, but citizens, too, had a duty to assist and a compelling interest in national security. The hair on the back of her neck stood on end. She didn't know exactly why.

"This is a special case because so much either initiated at the Nest or occurred here. Crawford having access, and now both Dayton and Lieutenant Blake being insiders and indisputably involved in the Crane and David Pace murders…I can't just haul them into a military court."

"Dayton knows too much," Madison said. A vice had to know everything. If anything happened to the commander, the vice had to be prepared to step in and not miss a beat.

"That's part of it." Talbot rocked forward, half leaned on his desk. "I've had doubts about him, so I've withheld everything I could withhold and still remain functional."

"What brought about those doubts?" Madison asked.

"Actually, you did." He almost smiled. "Your persistence about the satellite images on the David Pace matter. I thought if you were pushing that hard, it wasn't to see what was in those images—it was to confirm what you already knew was in those images."

"You'd be right," Madison said. "Pace wasn't burned, was he? He was put in the car after it exploded, and it didn't explode where it was found."

"Right on all counts."

"The physical evidence didn't hold up with the public story, so the cases were sealed."

"That's correct. The forensics told a very different story."

"So where did David Pace die?"

"In the woods on the Nest's perimeter, about ten meters from your favorite observation point."

She had the grace to blush. "I see."

His eyes sparkled, but he refrained from saying more

and shifted back to his original topic. "Because I could no longer trust Dayton, I had to lean more heavily on Renée. She has access to a continuity log and a disclosure letter for my replacement, in case of an emergency."

"Mrs. Renault?" Grant stiffened in his seat. "But she's a civilian outside the chain of command."

Talbot leveled his gaze. "She was a commander's wife for two decades, she has the necessary clearances, and after her husband's death I've made sure those clearances remained intact and current."

That was news to Madison, but not wholly surprising. Mrs. Renault had always been very devoted to the troops. "Why did you do that?"

Talbot's voice softened. "There are things that occur at an installation that a spouse knows and more one intuits. Though we'd prefer to insulate them entirely, that's not practical or even possible. This was recognized some time ago, and leadership determined that ignorance endangered them most, so a limited amount of information is disclosed to best protect them and give spouses what they need to protect themselves. There are considerable security considerations that factor in."

Madison knew this to be true. More often than the public realized, attempts to influence commanders were attempted through threats on their families.

Talbot thumbed the edge of his cup. "When my wife died, with John Renault's permission, I asked Renée if she'd be a surrogate and do for me and my troops what she did for her husband's—the professional duties of a commander's spouse. It was asking a lot, yet she graciously agreed."

"But you weren't even stationed here then." Madison worked to wrap her mind around this.

"No, I wasn't. But commanders are a close-knit group," he said. "Who better understands us or our challenges than each other? And who else can we talk to about them? No one."

Madison certainly saw the truth in that. "I see your point."

He craned back his head, lifting his chin. "Renée did a wonderful job, even long-distance. Do you know she flew to my headquarters every three months to meet with the spouses and encourage the troops?"

"No, sir. I didn't know that." Madison knew back then that Mrs. Renault took frequent trips, because she wouldn't be at church. But when she asked about her, everyone said she'd gone to visit family. And in a sense, Madison supposed she had—her military family.

Talbot's voice softened. "She seemed to know everything about everyone—their children, their troubles, what was most on their minds. Everyone adored Renée…including me." He paused, as if reliving fond memories, and then added, "After John died and I took over the command here, I offered to find someone else, but Renée said there was no need. She'd be happy to continue. I think it made her feel still connected to her military family and to John, and of course it was extremely beneficial to me. Grant can tell you. She's revered by the troops here."

"She is in a league of her own with all of them."

Talbot lowered his voice. "Frankly, I was relieved that she was willing to carry on. Renée is a remarkable asset, and I trust her."

He didn't come across as being in love with her, though until now, Madison and everyone else in North Bay believed he was. It was more like deep admiration and respect—almost hero worship.

Madison didn't know quite what to make of that, but it struck her as odd. Not the admiration and respect. That she totally understood. But hero worship?

Something was off there. She filed a mental note to revisit the matter when she could focus fully on it. "So what is the problem, sir?"

"Dayton and Blake." Talbot lifted a hand. "Regardless which one of them we're discussing, many of the crimes committed, including the murders of Beth Crane and David Pace, were committed in civilian communities and not on military installations. That gives civilian authorities jurisdiction. Yet it's vital to national security that we not release either Dayton or Blake to civilians."

"Blue Shoes's crimes take in the breadth of the country," Madison said. He'd launched multiple attacks on Maggie Mason from multiple states, and on Della Jackson also.

"Yes, they do."

"But you can't take them to military court, either?" Grant asked. "Courts-martial?"

"If I do, both will spill their guts about the Nest." Talbot frowned.

“Problematic either way.” Grant looked at Madison.

No way would the powers that be over the Nest and above Talbot allow either of those two options to happen. Madison had no doubt about that. “So you’re at odds on what to do with them.”

“Actually, that part of this has been resolved. Both men will remain in custody here.” He rubbed at his temple. “The problem is that they’re citizens as well as soldiers. I can’t hold them without a trial.”

They were entitled to due process, and nothing in Madison could ignore their rights and be at peace about it.

“What about a military tribunal?” Grant asked. “A case could be made for one based on the special circumstances. Enemy combatants?”

“A case has been made, but because of the nature of the special circumstances, leadership decided against a tribunal. The bean counters put the odds of a leak on the Nest at ninety percent.”

In Madison’s mind, the bean counters had been conservative. The case would leak. The accused or its counsel would see to it. “So what has leadership decided to do?” Clearly, the decision already had been made. This discussion with her and Grant wasn’t to reach a decision; it was to inform them of one. Why that was necessary Madison hadn’t yet concluded.

“Leadership wants a pretrial consensus. They’ll review determinations and findings and, if they agree that sufficient protections are afforded the men, they’ll hold a closed trial at their level and render a verdict for us to enforce."

"A pretrial consensus." Madison had been exposed to a lot in the legal world, but nothing like this. "What exactly is that?"

Talbot nodded. "Vetted individuals familiar with the case review the evidence, hear from the defendants and render conclusions based on the merits."

"Merits of the charges?" Madison asked.

"Conclusions on all of it—charges, evidence, testimony of the defendants—everything—in the form of a report on determinations and findings. That's where we run into a substantial challenge." Talbot's eyes clouded. "Dayton claims Blake is Blue Shoes. Blake says Dayton is Blue Shoes. Frankly, I don't think Blake is sharp enough. Dayton is plenty sharp, but I don't think he's crazy enough to do the things Blue Shoes has done, going all the way back to Della Jackson's case."

Blue Shoes had made several attempts to kill Della and set up her ex-husband, Jeff Jackson, to take the fall. Subsequently, the serial killer, Gary Crawford, had confessed to those crimes. "Blue Shoes wasn't exactly sane on Maggie Mason's case, either." He'd blown up an outdoor Christmas tree, put dud bomb collars on her dog and her uncle and set bombs inside a church to blow up on Christmas Eve. And all those things Crawford also had claimed credit for doing, but over time the facts had proven to Madison that, while Crawford had committed some crimes against Maggie, Blue Shoes had committed more. That, too, had been by Blue Shoes's design, and Crawford had confessed to everything, including killing Beth Crane and David Pace, to up his legendary status.

Talbot took a long drink of water from a bottle on his desk. "Since we can't disclose a thing to outsiders, leadership is retaining jurisdiction and has ordered both men be detained at the Nest."

"No hearings at all will occur," Grant concluded. When Talbot nodded, Grant grimaced. "Can we do that legally?"

"The joint chiefs and attorney general agree that we can and must. They've conferred with the president and he's signed off on it. I agreed with the stipulation that directives and specific orders based on our determinations and findings are issued and endorsed by all three."

It was an effective cover-your-back stipulation to protect Talbot. "Does that stipulation extend to those working with you to develop the determinations and findings?" Surely he wouldn't cover himself and hang his men out to dry.

He nodded. "Specifically stated. Everyone here is covered."

"By what authority is leadership doing this? Executive privilege?" Madison guessed.

"Probably an executive order," Grant said. "Or would he take a different venue, signing as Commander-in-Chief?"

"I wasn't told, and honestly I don't care," Talbot said. "If all three agree it's legal, I'm going to take it as legal."

Fair in Madison's view, since getting those three entities to agree on much of anything was always a steep mountain to climb and the Military Code of Justice no doubt didn't cite situations that fit these highly unusual circumstances. "What about Congress and the Supreme Court? Were they consulted?"

Talbot looked her right in the eye. "I have no idea. But I'd be shocked if all three signed off without consults. In their positions, I wouldn't."

"Are you allowed to consult with the JAG?" Grant asked.

"I'm expressly limited to the need-to-know loop."

Madison hadn't foreseen the special challenges in a trial, but she had wondered where Dayton and Blake would be held long term. The Nest was the logical choice. Leavenworth likely had been considered, but transfers there would require long-term isolation in solitary confinement, and even then the leaks were a rational fear. There were always leaks. The need-to-know loop would never deliberately risk that. Not with the Nest in the middle of all this.

Grant propped his ankle on his knee, then rested his hand on top. "So why are we here?" He motioned between Madison and himself. "What exactly do you want us to do?"

"It's substantial," Talbot warned them. "Informally depose everyone involved—Della, Maggie, Paul Mason and Ian Crane—and anyone else you need to, match out the evidence and build the case. I'll do what I can, but my ability to move freely is hampered—"

"By your position." It was. Not only was he military, but also the commander, and he'd be enforcing the decisions made by leadership based on the outcome. He needed distance from the report. "Basically," Madison cut to the chase, "you want us to build the case without letting anyone involved know we're building the case?"

Talbot nodded. "It's a huge task and we need to move rapidly to avoid legitimate complaints."

"Sir, I think speedy trials are the least of the worries here."

"It's a matter of what is right, Grant. Leadership is trying to be fair and protect the interests of the nation. It needs the truth so that someone isn't parked in isolation who doesn't belong there."

Sacrificed. Madison blinked hard.

"Since both men are in the military and their rights aren't as restrictive as those for civilians, we have more latitude, but that compels us to be more diligent. We need a compelling, decisive package."

Grant looked at Madison. When she nodded her agreement, he told Talbot, "We'll develop a strategy and run it past you before moving on it."

Talbot stood up. "I know you two will do your best. In fact, I'm counting on it."

He was, Madison realized. For himself and for Beecher. Leadership was holding him totally responsible for all that had happened. She frowned. "Sir, has this jeopardized your promotion?"

"That promotion is insignificant to me, Madison. My reputation rests on the outcome of your investigation."

He shrugged, and then smiled. "I'm confident I'm in competent hands."

Madison clasped Talbot's hand. "We'll do our best."

"That's all anyone can ask."

She and Grant left Talbot's office, spoke briefly to Beecher and then, on the way downstairs, Madison checked behind her to make sure the stairwell was clear. Discovering that it was, she asked Grant, "Was he talking about our hands being competent?"

"Maybe, but he might have been reaching a little higher."

"God?"

Grant shrugged. "That's where I'd be reaching." He paused on the landing. "If this investigation doesn't go well, his career is history."

Madison sobered and looked Grant in the eye, pausing on the stair above the landing. "I'm glad to hear that—not about his career, but that you'd be reaching to God. And it doesn't hurt to know that Talbot isn't just a seat-warmer in church. You know what I mean."

Grant sent her a puzzled look. "Not really."

"I've come to respect him. Mrs. Renault has feelings for him that run a lot deeper than she admits. His feelings for her trouble me a little, but it's good to know he's a godly man."

"What's your point?"

"Hero worship. It's natural in some cases, but for a man in his position…I've never seen it."

"He's still human, Madison. He should respect and

admire Mrs. Renault. She's gone the extra mile for him for years."

"I know." What exactly was troubling her about that? She couldn't peg it. "But something there isn't…quite right."

"He feels guilty for being in love with her."

"I thought so, too," she admitted, gripping the metal banister. No doubt, his relationship with John Renault factored into that. "Now, I'm not so sure that's it."

"*It* what?" Grant asked. "What are you saying, Madison?"

"I don't know—yet. I've just got this feeling. Something doesn't sit quite right. I'm not saying it's bad or good, just that something there is not as it should be."

"But you respect him. Does that mean you've forgiven him for detaining you?"

They stepped outside. A gush of crisp air slapped Madison in the face. She nodded, and brushed a hank of hair out of her eyes. "He was doing what he had to do, and I'll tell you a secret I discovered during that exchange we just left."

"What?"

"He didn't detain me because he thought I was guilty. He detained me to protect me from Dayton."

"You're likely right about that, but what made you decide that in this meeting?"

Madison struggled to streamline her sinuous thoughts. "He knows Dayton and Blake are guilty, and yet he's giving them the benefit of doubt. He doesn't want to be wrong, or to see them sacrificed."

Dawning lit in Grant's eyes. "No one is to be lost."

"Exactly."

Grant unlocked the door to his Jeep and they climbed inside. "When he ordered me to infiltrate your agency, he didn't say he was being protective, but his questions and orders took that slant. I wasn't sure if that was true or just me wanting it to be true."

Madison shut the door and then buckled her safety belt. "I think he'd sacrifice himself before he hurt Mrs. Renault. If he thought I was a danger to her, he'd have jerked her out of my reach so fast, her head would still be spinning."

Grant paused, then grunted. "I hadn't thought of that, but I agree."

Madison lifted her hands. "So where do we start?"

"Background." He buckled up. "Where else?"

"Then I need thinking fuel."

"What kind?" Grant cranked the ignition.

"Key lime pie from Miss Addie's—it's the best. And coffee. If no one else can know what we're doing and time is of the essence, then you realize we're going to be pulling a lot of late nights."

"Works for me."

She smiled. She couldn't help it. The idea of spending a lot more time with Grant appealed…even if the work was grim and daunting.

Madison and Grant holed up at Madison's mansion on the bay. The house fronted on the water and was open and airy, decorated with lots of cushy pillows and pastel colors. In the last North Bay Parade of Homes, it had been deemed stunning—and Madison agreed it was. She actually lived in a small section of the seven-thousand-square-foot home—the master suite, family room, kitchen and her downstairs office. The rest was just there. "Let's set up in the dining room," she told Grant.

"Won't all the stuff be in your way?"

"Not at all. I only use the dining room for parties or when my sorority sisters gather here. It's too big and formal for me. I like the kitchen."

"It's an intimidating house."

"It is?" Genuinely surprised, she grunted.

"I didn't mean it was cold. It's obviously a home. It's just huge."

"Yeah, it is. Crazy for just one person, isn't it?"

"Not if you like it."

"I like the dock." She glanced through French doors beyond the lawn to the wooden dock that stretched out into the water. "The house came with it."

"Ah."

That didn't seem to surprise him at all. Madison was glad about that.

While he hauled in the records and files Talbot had released to them as relevant, she phoned Mrs. Renault.

"Lost, Inc. How may I direct your call?"

"Mrs. Renault, it's Madison." In the kitchen, she leaned a hip against the sand-colored granite counter.

"Are you on vacation, visiting friends or eloping with Grant?"

Madison nearly choked. "What?"

"How should I explain your absences around here?"

Talbot had already talked to the woman. Probably before he'd talked to them. *Eloping with Grant.* The idea held more appeal than was likely healthy for them. "I was thinking more along the lines of we're working on a case."

"Which one?"

"You don't know." That would shock the others. They'd spend more time talking about Mrs. Renault being unaware than what Madison and Grant were doing.

"Oh, my. You are pulling out all the stops."

Madison chuckled. "Your friend is counting on us. I don't want to disappoint him or you."

Silence.

Strange, but Madison let it stretch.

"Reveal the truth, Madison, and let the chips fall where they may," Mrs. Renault finally said. Sadness tinted her tone.

It puzzled Madison. She watched Grant set a box of files on the floor near the wall within a couple arms' reach. "Are you trying to tell me something?"

"You know, dear, the truth is often obscured by half-truths and preconceived notions. I suggest you abandon them and start fresh with none."

There was a message there. And it wasn't a positive one.

The line went dead.

Thoughtful, Madison hung up the phone.

Carrying another box from where Beecher had deposited them at the front door into the dining room, Grant paused. "What's wrong?"

"Nothing." She frowned and motioned with her hand. "I'm not sure."

"Are you sick? You look kind of pale all of a sudden."

"No. No, I'm fine." She was probably making too much of this. "I just spoke with Mrs. Renault. She's telling everyone that we're working on a case—she doesn't know which one." No way would Madison mention that eloping business to him.

"What about that's upset you?"

"Nothing. It's what she said after." Madison turned to fully face Grant. "It was a warning, Grant."

He set the box down and walked closer. "What kind of warning? About what?"

"She knows what we're doing. I surmised Talbot had already called her. She said to reveal the truth. That it was obscured by half-truths and preconceived notions and she advised that we drop them and started fresh." Madison swept her hair back from her face. "I think she's worried we're going to lose the truth because we'll see what we expect to see."

"Or fail to see what we should." He parked a hand on his hip. "She wouldn't get more specific?"

Madison shook her head.

"Well, she's not the type to say anything lightly. So we keep this firmly in mind and do what we've got to do."

"Just like that?"

"Just like what?"

"You accept her warning just like that?"

"Of course. This is Mrs. Renault, Madison. She'd never misguide you or me, and no one is more protective of the troops." Grant turned and picked up the box. "If she knows something and isn't sharing it, she's got reason. If we miss it, my guess is she'll somehow put it in our path so we fall over it. We just have to have open minds."

She probably would…if she could. "What if she can't put it in our paths? She's got insights but she'd never breach security."

Grant squared the stack of boxes to the others, then turned to Madison, dusting his hands. "Then we'd better not miss the signs."

"Such a wise man."

"Are you getting testy with me?" Grant seemed pleased by that. He grabbed her and growled into her neck.

"That's going to cost you," she promised, smiling up at him.

"I'll pay." He pecked a kiss to her lips. "Good to see you getting back to normal."

"Normal? What do you mean?"

"You've been walking on eggshells. It's good to see your feet on the ground again."

"Not eggshells. In the clouds." She let out a delicate laugh. "I've just been…happy."

"Healing."

She stilled, sniffed, totally captivated by him. “That, too,” she admitted. “We’d better get started.”

His eyes warmed. “Yeah. Della Jackson’s case? It happened first. But let’s set up a system first.”

Madison grabbed a dry-erase board. “I do love a man who appreciates order.”

“Is that all it takes to please you?”

He wanted to please her. Moved, she admitted the truth. “Not all, but it goes a long way.”

Grant smiled. “Good to know.”

By eight-thirty that night, they had transformed the dining room.

The far wall stood covered with photographs and pages with question marks for unidentified persons of interest and blank space to add more. The south wall, facing the water, was labeled “timelines,” where they would insert color-coded verifications of who was where and when. The east wall no longer held a giant mirror and magnificent oil paintings. On it hung a huge dry-erase board, where they would enter crimes they believed had been committed by Blue Shoes with the relevant data, and on the west wall, they’d hung a giant map of the United States and to its left, a map of North Bay and the surrounding area. There, with colored pins, they’d peg the locations of crimes and verified whereabouts.

Madison stood back and reviewed what they’d accomplished. “So far, so good on getting things in order.” She glanced at Grant. “Hungry?”

"Let's get takeout." He stared at the seven boxes of files waiting for their review.

It wasn't what he said but the way he said it that snagged Madison's attention and raised an alert. "What's up with you?"

"I don't know," he said, his expression serious. He tugged at the crumpled cuff of his sleeve. "I just keep thinking we need to hurry. If we don't, we'll miss something significant."

"As in evidence disappearing?"

He blinked hard and fast. "Or maybe appearing."

His feeling resonated with her. She'd had an uneasy kind of strange feeling since Beecher had dropped off the files, though she hadn't pegged it in the exact way as Grant. How he'd react to what she'd next say, she had no idea. But clearly it was time she found out. "We need help."

"We can't call in anyone. You heard Talbot."

"I mean big-gun help. The biggest kind of help."

He looked baffled.

She held out her hands. "Pray with me, Grant. Would you do that?"

"I will." He clasped her hands, gently squeezed and bowed his head.

It was one of the most beautiful moments of her life. And even as it happened, she knew she'd cherish the memory of it for a lifetime.

EIGHT

By two o'clock on Saturday, content on the wallboards had taken shape on Della Jackson's case. The timeline had been constructed, the crimes pinned on the map, and related photos were up. One question mark with a yellow line, signifying Della's case, hung on the photo board. It represented an unknown mentioned in a report faxed over from Della, but never mentioned again.

Grant sat sprawled in a chair at the table, reviewing the report for the umpteenth time, and Madison sat across from him, reviewing the supporting documents Talbot had accumulated on Della's case.

Only the ticking clock broke the silence as they scoured the documents.

Madison finished and stretched, then refilled their tall glasses of sweet tea. When she returned, Grant sat staring at the closed file. "We've got to ask her."

"Yes." She set the glass down on the table near him. "I'll do it." It would come across more natural than if it came from Grant.

Madison grabbed her phone and made the call. When

it rang, she engaged the speakerphone so Grant could hear the conversation, too.

"Della, it's Madison."

"Hi, stranger. Where've you been?"

"Don't ask," Madison said, trying to forestall any more questions she didn't want to answer about what she was doing. "Remember during your ordeal, that incident outside the Boat House restaurant with the skateboarder?"

"Of course. Why?"

"Your report mentioned that he'd been paid to plant a little plastic mailbox in your purse, but you didn't say who he was. I need to know."

"Tommy Jasper," she said. "Paul and I went and talked to him and his father, Pete."

"The boy couldn't identify the man who'd paid him?"

"We showed him photos of suspects—Jeff Jackson and Crawford—but neither of them were the guy. He did say he was fit and could have been military—short haircut. He also said the guy had kept his tan. That struck Tommy as odd because it was October."

"You have an address on him?"

"Tommy? Yes. Hold on."

Madison met Grant's gaze. "It's a long shot, but..." Mrs. Renault's warning stuck in Madison's mind. At the end of this, she wanted no stone left unturned and no regrets.

Della came back on the line and reeled off the address, Tommy's father's name, and then said, "First you wanted the report and now this. Madison, what is going on?"

"Nothing. I'm just wrapping up some paperwork."

"And I'm stunt-flying in a hurricane," Della challenged her. "Did Crawford recant his confession?"

"Not that I know of." Apparently word hadn't yet filtered out that Crawford was dead. There had to be a reason the news remained suppressed so Madison didn't reveal it. "I've got to run now."

"But wait. If this involves me, I should—"

"Don't worry, Della. Everything is fine."

"Okay." Still hesitant, Della sought reassurance. "But if it gets to a point where it's not fine, you'll tell me, right?"

Madison wanted her friend to rest easy. To enjoy her new life and marriage to Paul Mason without the past haunting either of them. "I will," Madison said, and prayed she hadn't just promised something she couldn't deliver. "Bye."

She hung up the phone. Grant was pulling photos down from the board. "What are you doing?"

"Getting visuals for Tommy. Maybe he'll be able to identify the man who paid him."

Madison grabbed her purse. In the garage, she grabbed a small ice chest.

"What's that for?"

"We're driving right by the Seafood Mart." She shrugged. "I thought we'd have a shrimp boil for supper."

"Sounds good."

* * *

Madison drove past the Boat House restaurant, then turned left to get to Grandview Avenue. When she pulled onto it, she slowed down to look for the street numbers on the mailboxes at the edge of the road.

"There it is." Grant pointed to a brick ranch.

Madison pulled in at the curb. A red truck sat parked in the driveway, and across the street, a man raked leaves and dumped them into a wheelbarrow.

"Pretty area." Grant unbuckled, then checked his watch. "It's nearly four. Looks like someone's at home."

"Pete," Madison said. "Tommy's dad. He drives the red truck." A for-sale sign hung taped to the back window. Madison dumped her keys into her handbag and walked with Grant up the narrow sidewalk to the front door. She rang the bell and heard the chimes sound deep inside.

Tommy answered. Flaming red hair, thin and wiry, wearing a T-shirt that read Skateboarding Is Not a Crime and shorts that hung past his knees. He had a copy of *Skateboard Science* in his hand. "Yeah?"

"Tommy, I'm Madison McKay and this is Grant Deaver."

"Dad?" he called back over his shoulder. "Some people are here about the truck."

Madison waited until a man who had to be Pete came to the door. He was brawny, with beefy arms and the same flaming red hair as Tommy, though Pete was going gray at the temples. "Afternoon."

"Good afternoon," Madison said. "We're not here about the truck, Mr. Jasper."

His eyes widened. "What do you want, then?"

Grant stepped closer to the door. "Actually, we wanted to talk with Tommy."

Pete Jasper sent his son a sidelong look. "You been riding that board where you shouldn't, son?"

"No, sir."

Pete looked at Grant. "What do you want to talk to Tommy about?"

Madison touched Grant's sleeve. "Mr. Jasper, do you remember Della Jackson?"

Tommy cringed. "Whatever it is, I didn't do it."

Madison smiled. Apparently the boy had learned his lesson about working for someone he didn't know. "We don't think you did something wrong, Tommy. We're just trying to close up some files."

"I read in the paper where they caught that stalker," Pete said. "Gary Crawford. A cold-blooded killer, and my boy was that close to him." Spreading his fingers an inch, Pete Jasper shivered.

"It was something," Grant said. "Glad you weren't hurt, Tommy."

"Me, too."

"So what do you need, Ms. McKay?" Pete, not Tommy, asked.

"I know Tommy looked at some photos for Della, trying to identify the man who hired him."

Tommy came forward. "Yes, ma'am. But he wasn't the one they arrested. He didn't look at all like him."

"Would you mind taking a look at a few more photos for us?" Grant pulled the pictures out of his pocket.

Tommy looked confused. "Sure, but what for? It's the same guy."

He had just said they didn't look anything alike. Madison stilled, confused. "What do you mean?"

"Ms. Jackson asked us to keep an eye out. I think she was scared he might come after me or something—you know, because I saw him. So we did watch for him."

"That's right." Pete crossed his chest with his arms.

"I saw him in the newspaper." Tommy looked at his dad.

"He sure did. I called it in right away."

"To Della Jackson?"

"No." Pete looked at Grant. "He was wearing a military uniform, so I called out to the base. Told them all about it."

Madison and Grant exchanged a wary glance. "Who did you talk to out there? Do you know?"

"Well, I got the regular number out of the phone book. They said they were transferring me to the..." He paused. "I can't recollect."

"Information officer?" Grant suggested.

"I guess. I really don't recall, but it doesn't matter anyway. They put me straight through to the commander's office."

Grant shifted his weight on his feet. "You talked to Commander Talbot, then?"

"I don't recall his name, but it was the commander's office."

Could have been Dayton or Blake. Most likely Blake, Madison thought. He typically fielded Talbot's calls.

"So what happened?"

"I told him everything that had happened and that Tommy had seen a picture of the guy who'd hired him in the paper."

Boy, it'd make things easier if Pete knew whom he'd talked to then. "Okay." Madison motioned to Grant. "Let's get Tommy to look at the pictures."

"I don't need to look at 'em." Tommy hiked a thumb and motioned inside the house. "I can get you the picture from the paper if you want."

"You kept it?" Madison was surprised.

"I thought I'd better. If he decided to come back, I wanted my mom and dad to not forget what he looked like. It's hanging on the fridge."

"We'd appreciate seeing it, Tommy," Grant said.

Tommy disappeared into the house and the three adults waited on the stoop. "Is he loose?" Pete's bright eyes filled with worry.

"We'll know in a minute," Grant told him.

Tommy returned. "Here it is." He passed the newspaper clipping to Madison.

She looked at his familiar face, scanned up to the date on the newspaper. "Dayton."

Grant grunted. "Yes, it is."

"That's what I told them at the commander's office. He hired Tommy, so we figured he was the one stalking Della Jackson."

"Thank you very much," Grant said. "May I take a picture of this?" He lifted the curled-edge article.

Pete nodded.

Grant snapped a few shots with his phone's camera, making sure Tommy was in two of them.

Madison extended her hand. "Thank you very much."

"Is this guy out of play now?" Pete asked.

She wished she could reassure him, but she couldn't. "I don't know his disposition, Mr. Jasper. I'm sorry."

That was a finer line between the truth and not than she cared to walk, especially knowing the man was worried about his son's safety, but she honestly didn't know Dayton's disposition yet. She hated for them to feel they needed to be on guard, but she hated more the idea of them not being guarded and needing to be. Was Dayton working alone? Did he have help? Who knew—yet?

They left the Jasper house and got into the car. When the doors closed, Grant buckled, then looked over at her. "Who got that call at the commander's office?"

"I would think Blake."

"So would I." Grant worried his lip. "Talbot doesn't know it, or he would have shared it."

Would he? "One would think." Madison weighed both sides. "Blake could have taken the call and transferred it to Dayton."

"Or taken it himself, noted and forgotten it."

"Possible." Madison waited for a woman pushing a stroller down the street to pass, then pulled away from the curb. "Blake might have dismissed it. Della's case didn't have a military connection."

Grant frowned. "Apparently it did. We just didn't know it until now."

At the corner, Madison stopped. The smell of someone's backyard barbecue filtered into the car. She turned on the highway and headed toward the Seafood Mart. "So Della's ex, Jeff Jackson, was arrested for everything on her case. Then a couple of months later, Gary Crawford is arrested, and he confesses to most of the crimes against Della." An odd tingle started at the base of Madison's spine. "What's the date on that newspaper with the photo of Dayton?" She'd looked at it but couldn't for the life of her remember it.

Grant pulled out his phone and checked the photo. "January 4."

"So on January 4, Pete Jasper calls the commander's office and reveals Dayton was involved in Della's case," Madison said, letting that information fall into place.

"The phone call—not the fear of Crawford recanting—is what sealed Crawford's fate." Grant adjusted the heater vent.

"Maybe. If Blake took Pete's call and knew Dayton had been identified, then he could make that evidence go away, and Dayton would owe him." Madison could see Blake doing that. Leverage to feed his ambition.

Grant saw something different. "Or Blake transferred the call from Pete Jasper directly to Dayton, and he buried it."

"That makes even more sense," Madison said.

"Why?"

She pulled into the Seafood Mart, parked and looked over at Grant. "Because Tommy Jasper is still alive and so is his father. If Blake was using the call as leverage against Dayton, Dayton would have eliminated the leverage."

"He would have. Likely he'd have eliminated Blake, too." Grant grimaced. "Dayton got the call."

Madison lifted the cooler. "That's the most logical conclusion." She reached for her door. "With everything he'd done, I can't see Dayton leaving witnesses or anyone in place who could implicate him in any crime."

"Neither can I." Grant squeezed her hand. "After dinner we'll take a look at Maggie's case. Maybe something that ties to Dayton will show up there."

"Maybe it will."

The house held the pungent smell of Zatarain's Shrimp and Crab Boil. Grant prepared new potatoes and mini ears of corn on the cob while Madison rinsed the shrimp. Soft jazz floated through the kitchen.

Grant scrubbed the vegetables and dropped them in a colander. "I didn't know you were a jazz fan."

Madison nodded. "Since my first trip to New Orleans."

"I knew you were a fan of the city, just not the music."

"How?" She tumbled the shrimp in the strainer, let the water flow through her fingertips.

"The Zatarain's was a dead giveaway." He smiled.

"If you weren't a New Orleans fan, you'd likely use Old Bay."

He finished cleaning the vegetables. "Should I put them in the pot?"

"Yes." She blinked hard. The intense spices had her eyes tearing.

"The Saints emblem on the wall in the family room was probably a hint, too. And the mug." He grinned. "Minnie's jealous."

"Minnie's for at work. She counters all the bad stuff I hear about there. The Saints are for at home."

They chatted while the potatoes and corn boiled and Madison combined horseradish and ketchup to make a dipping sauce for the shrimp. "Do you want rémoulade sauce, too?"

"No. I like the red."

Madison smiled. "Me, too."

Grant grunted. "We have a lot in common."

They did. And now they were both discovering it, and that was a good thing. Madison had been concerned about how she and Grant would mesh and get along once the trauma embroiling them was over. Crises could forge bonds that fell apart as soon as the crises ended. She didn't want to fall into that trap, which was why she wouldn't let Grant explain himself after her release from the Nest. She needed to see how they were together when they weren't in crisis. True, they were far from calm with so much on the line in their work, but that would always be the case. With the military and working at Lost, Inc., pressure and high stakes were part of the job. But it was different than secrets coming between them, or being divided by conflicts.

So far, having time together—even if they were focused on work—had been a good thing. *Very good.* Tempted to pinch herself, she dumped the strainer of seafood into the boiling water. The shells instantly turned bright coral.

"Madison, can I tell you something?"

Rinsing the strainer, she glanced at Grant. "Sure."

"I'd rather be neck-deep in serious trouble with you than anywhere else without you."

She tilted her head. A man wearing an apron holding a red scrubber held an amazing amount of appeal. "Did that come out wrong?"

"I don't think so." He noted her lips twitching. "You're teasing me. Are you teasing me?"

She laughed. "I am."

He dipped his chin, looked down at her. "You know what happens when you tease me?"

"I'm hoping I'll get a kiss," she said. Laughing, he folded her in his arms.

Madison dropped the strainer in the sink and melted into his embrace.

When he pulled back, he sucked in a sharp, staggered breath.

She left him breathless—and loved knowing it. "Why don't you get some newspaper and spread it on the table on the patio."

"What for?"

"Have you never had a proper seafood boil?"

"Apparently not."

"Oh, then you are in for a treat." She waved him to the patio. "Spread the paper. Cover the whole table."

An hour later, they still sat at the newspaper-covered table, its center piled high with shrimp shells. They'd smeared butter and sour cream on the potatoes and corn. The spices had made them hot and delicious—a treat to the taste buds.

"This was a great idea," Grant said. "I don't think I'll ever see a plain potato the same way again."

It was warm out; pleasant with a light breeze that didn't carry a chill. "I enjoyed it, too. But I ate way too much."

He nodded toward the bay. "The water's calm. Pretty." He stood up, looked out then back to her. "I see why you love the dock. The view's amazing." He started clearing the table.

"No, no." Madison waved him off. "Take the condiments in and bring out the trash can."

He did and then stood waiting.

Madison took the can, and shoved the whole mess into it. "Done."

Grant laughed. "That's my kind of cleanup."

"Fabulous, isn't it?" She giggled.

"Before we go back to work, let's walk down on the pier."

"Okay. Just need to wash my hands first."

"Good idea."

Minutes later, they walked down the five steps to the dock, then strolled out over the water.

Madison looked at the twinkling lights across the harbor. "This is why I bought this place."

"Like I said, amazing view." He stepped up behind her and hugged her. "You love the water—your favorite place at the club is by the water, too."

"It's transparent. You can trust what you see."

"Ah."

They stood and stargazed a long while, content just being there together.

"Madison?" Grant said softly. "Do you think…" he started, stopped, then tried again. "One day, do you think you can get past what I did and really forgive me?"

"I told you." She turned in his arms. "I already have."

"Would I be crazy to hope that one day you could more than forgive me?"

So vulnerable and unsure. It moved her. "No more crazy than me. I—I—" A boat's horn blasted. She turned back to the water. "Want to come to church with me tomorrow?"

"Yes." He chuckled. "I've been wondering if you were going to give me a hard time about breaking from work to go."

"Not me." She leaned back into him. "I know Talbot needs our findings as soon as possible, but priorities are priorities."

"I'm taking it you're not mad at God anymore."

She looked back over her shoulder at him, genuinely surprised. "How did you know I was angry with God? I didn't really know it."

"I'm not sure. I just knew."

"Interesting." She laced their fingers. "I was wrong, regardless. I thought He'd abandoned me, too. But then it hit me. Whatever I needed, came into my path. It was beyond strange, Grant. When I realized how often that had happened..."

"You knew only He could orchestrate it?"

"Exactly. Of course, then I felt like forty kinds of fool for not realizing it before then."

"I hear you on that. Seems we all do it all the time."

"I guess." She sure did.

Grant let out a contented sigh. "This has been a perfect day."

With grace, she hoped it was the first of many perfect days. They had made a lot of progress, and she was grateful for it. The adversarial relationship between them was gone. The question was, what relationship would they build to replace it?

Maggie Mason's case was more complex than Della Jackson's.

An FBI profiler, Madison's best friend, Maggie Mason, had been called in on the serial killer, now murder victim, Gary Crawford's case. She'd gotten too close to catching him, and he'd spent the next three years trying to punish her for it by making Maggie his fifth victim. He'd come dangerously close to succeeding multiple times. The worst, by far, was an incident in Utah that had landed Maggie in the hospital for months.

Finally, Crawford had been apprehended and had

confessed to David Pace's and Beth Crane's murders along with a string of other crimes.

Working nonstop until Tuesday afternoon, Grant and Madison had wrestled with the timeline, the photos, and pinned the map, color-coding the entries red to differentiate them from the yellow ones that pertained to Della Jackson's case.

No conflicts were evident.

"I'm stumped." Madison slumped back in her chair. "It appears Crawford actually did do all of this."

"Maybe he did." Grant frowned and tugged at his sweater sleeve. It had gotten chilly again, a crisp forty-five degrees. "Did you read this report about the kids' Christmas program?"

"What about it?" Madison took a sip of hot chocolate. "I know Crawford planted bombs in the church, but Beecher disarmed them. They ended up holding the Christmas program in the parking lot at Miss Addie's Café."

"I'm talking about the part in Maggie Mason's report where she says Gracie—I'm guessing that's Miss Addie's granddaughter, Gracie—was given a black rose by an unidentified male who told her to give it to Maggie."

"Uh-huh, it was that Gracie, and that's right. Crawford had a thing for black roses. That's how Maggie knew to get everyone out of the church."

"Did Gracie ever identify the man?"

"She didn't know him—I'm going from memory here, not the report. After Crawford was apprehended,

Miss Addie took Gracie down to the station to take a look at Crawford, but she said he wasn't the man who gave her the rose."

Grant mulled that over. "She knows Talbot and Dayton, right?"

Madison shrugged. "I can't say for sure, but she doesn't miss much and they're in the café all the time. I'd think she knows them."

Grant looked up from the report in his hand. "Is Blake at Miss Addie's Café all the time, too?"

Madison inhaled near her cup, seemingly enjoying the hot chocolate's scent as much as its taste, and, gauging from her darting eyes, she was scanning her own memory. With Miss Addie's Café being so close to the agency, Madison was a regular. Had she ever seen Blake there?

"Seems strange that he wouldn't be known there—everyone in North Bay ends up at Miss Addie's at some time—but I don't believe I've ever seen him there so I don't know about Gracie."

A bubble formed in Grant's gut. If Madison hadn't seen Blake, maybe Gracie hadn't, either. "Let's go find out."

Miss Addie was a birdlike woman with sharp features and kind eyes, and everyone agreed she was the best cook in four counties.

Madison and Grant, along with more than half of North Bay, were regulars, and headed for their usual table in the back near the door to the outside dining room. It was popular in summer but vacant during the winter months unless there was a warm, sunny day.

Today, it was raining. Hard.

Madison propped her umbrella in the stand by the door. It was too late for lunch and too early for dinner, but a couple dozen people had slipped in out of the rain for coffee and dessert.

Miss Addie spotted them and walked over. "Well, I ain't seen you two in a week. Thought you'd given me up for that new joint down the street using lacy tablecloths."

Grant looked bewildered. "There's a new joint down the street?" He started to rise. "We should check it out."

Miss Addie pushed down on his shoulder. "Park yourself, boy. I hear Pauline Colfax is their head cook."

"Pauline?" Madison couldn't believe it. "Why would anyone hire her to cook?"

"Beats me." Miss Addie dropped her voice. "The poor woman don't know a spoon from a spatula, and can't boil water. Bless her heart."

Grant grunted. "Maybe you should give her lessons."

She looked at him and grinned. "That would be the Christian thing to do, wouldn't it? Now, what can I get you today?" She scanned back over her shoulder. "I got red velvet cake, carrot cake— Whoops. Jack Sampson just snitched the last piece of carrot cake. Sorry. What else is over there, Gracie?"

The girl called out from the kitchen. "Apple pie and that crunchy blueberry stuff, Gran."

"I'll have the crunchy stuff." Madison grinned.

"No Key lime?" Grant was disappointed.

"Grant Deaver, you're gonna turn into a Key lime." She tsked at Madison. "I've never seen a man that loves it better."

"That's not a bad thing." Grant placed his napkin in his lap.

"Well, I had one put aside in the back to take home tonight, but I can spare you a piece."

Grant grinned. "You're a saint, Miss Addie."

"No, darlin', that I ain't. But I like a man who loves what he loves with his whole heart." She meandered to her kitchen.

Madison bit her lower lip.

"She's got a story to tell about that, doesn't she?"

"Unfortunately." Madison frowned at Grant. "Her husband went out for milk and bread and didn't come back. He left her with no money and no way to support herself and her daughter." Which explained why she made a point of warning girls never to put all their eggs in anyone else's basket, including Madison.

"How long ago?"

"Twenty or more years."

"Ouch."

"Yeah, ouch." Madison nodded, adding weight to her opinion. "She knew how to cook and clean. So she did a lot of both. Now she owns a bunch of rental cottages and the café."

"She's walked a hard road. Retiring will give her a chance to do what she wants to do rather than what she has to do to get by."

Madison smiled. "Miss Addie isn't going to retire, Grant."

"But she just said—"

"She'll teach Pauline because she has kids to feed and she can't cook. Without Miss Addie, Pauline will fail."

"So she'll help her competition succeed?"

Madison sent him an indulging look. "She will, but Pauline will no longer be Miss Addie's competition."

"She'll see she's in over her head and come to work here for Miss Addie."

Madison nodded.

Grant grunted. "Humph. She'll make it a win/win. Good for her and Pauline."

"Exactly."

Truth dawned in Grant's eyes. "She's done this before."

"Over the years, several times." Madison leaned close. "Miss Addie doesn't much care for competition on her street, either, which is probably why Pauline chose it. She can't cook but she knows Miss Addie."

Grant sat back. "Why not just come ask Miss Addie to help her?"

"Same reason Miss Addie didn't just offer to help her." Madison stiffened. "Pauline's got nothing left but a little dignity. Miss Addie doesn't want to take that away from her, too."

"Why is offering to help the woman taking her dignity?"

"Because it implies she can't do it on her own." Madison patted his hand on the table. "Don't worry. Miss Addie and Pauline know how it works here. They'll handle it, and Pauline will be working here by the end of the week."

"What about her lease on the other property, where she's opened her own place? It's not that easy to just shut the door."

"It is when Miss Addie owns the property."

Grant's jaw dropped.

Madison laughed.

"What's so funny?" Miss Addie returned with the pie and blueberry crunch.

"Nothing really. Grant was just getting a dose of insight on how Southern women think."

"We are a maze-minded bunch, I suppose." She set their dishes down.

"I need to talk with Gracie, Miss Addie. About the rose at the Christmas service."

"What for?"

"Just finishing off some paperwork." Madison lifted her fork.

Miss Addie's eyes narrowed. She wasn't buying that paperwork claim for a second. "I'll send her over after you enjoy your dessert." She filled their coffee cups.

"Talking about it won't upset her, will it?" Grant asked. "That was a pretty traumatic night."

"Shoot, all she ever talks about is getting to play Mary in the Christmas program and it being the only one ever held in the parking lot. She never mentions the scares that took place that night."

"Kids are resilient." Madison sank her fork into the hot blueberry crunch.

When the last bites had been eaten, Madison watched Gracie walk over to their table wearing jeans, a red sweater and a cherry-red nose. She'd been outside playing. Madison smiled. "I like your hair in a ponytail."

Gracie beamed. "It's brown. I wish it was silver-blond like your hair."

"Oh, brown hair is much prettier," Madison said, hoping Gracie never suffered a trauma that changed her hair color so dramatically. "You can wear any color you want." She leaned closer. "I have to be careful about that. Some colors just don't go well with silver-blond."

"Huh." Gracie looked at Grant. "You need a haircut."

He smiled. "I guess it is getting pretty shaggy. I just haven't had time to take care of it."

"Gran says we have to make time to take care of ourselves." She cocked her head. "She knows, 'cause she's old and everything."

"Ah." Grant kept a straight face. "Wise, too, I'd say."

"Very." Gracie nodded emphatically.

"Can I ask you to look at a picture or two for me, Gracie?" Madison reached into her purse.

"I like to look at pictures."

"Do you remember the man who gave you the black rose for Maggie the night of the Christmas program?"

She nodded, then told Grant, "I was Mary."

"The best Mary ever is what I heard."

"Thank you." Gracie beamed. "I practiced real hard."

"So you'll look at the pictures, then?" Madison asked.

Gracie nodded.

Madison put photos of Talbot and Dayton on the table.

"It wasn't them." She looked at Madison. "I know them. It was the man with the lawn mower."

Miss Addie joined them.

"What lawn mower?" Grant asked.

"The one across the street from our house."

Miss Addie clarified. "He was cutting the grass at one of my cottages across the street from Della's right before her garage blew up."

Madison and Grant exchanged a heavy look, and Madison's heart beat hard deep in her chest. She held out a third photo. "Gracie, do you recog—"

Gracie's face lit up. "That's him." She grabbed Miss Addie's arm. "Gran, that's the rose man with the lawn mower. He looks different without his hat, but that's him."

"Blake," Madison said.

"Blake?" Miss Addie looked from Madison to Grant and back to Madison. "Who is he?"

Obviously Blake didn't come into Miss Addie's. Madison gave the wise woman a warning look. "No one important. Just someone we ran into on another case."

That response had been given for Gracie's benefit. Miss Addie, indeed wise, sent Madison a worried look. "Gracie, go help in the kitchen for a bit, sweetie."

"Bye, Mr. Deaver. Madison." Gracie skipped from the dining room behind the door to the kitchen.

"Now I want to know the truth about this bit of business."

Madison knew determined when she saw it. "Make sure Gracie doesn't mention this to anyone, and don't you mention it, either. For now, that's all I'm free to tell you."

"Is he running loose?"

Madison didn't answer.

"Enough said." Miss Addie grabbed their plates. "You get him and keep him, Madison McKay. I ain't having that lowlife coming after my Gracie. I'll shoot him myself." She took the dishes to the kitchen.

Grant watched her go. "I think she'd do it."

"Bet on it."

They rose to go. Madison grabbed her umbrella. "I think we'd better do some deep background on Blake. He's showing up in all the wrong places."

"Talbot already has. You can be sure he put Blake through the mill before he got hired to work in the commander's office."

"Then we'd better rerun it and check out the background of whoever ran the check, because they evidently missed a few key things."

NINE

Wednesday was a bust. Thursday wasn't much better, and so far, Friday was proving to be just as fruitless. Grant and Madison had spent no less than fourteen hours per day digging into Lieutenant Blake's background and they had discovered nothing more than Blake was efficient and ambitious—neither of which were liabilities in the military realm unless he crossed the proverbial line, and from all accounts, he hadn't.

Blake's performance, gauged by his annual Officer Effectiveness Reports, was positive. The last three OERs all carried endorsements from two-star generals, including the last one from Commander Talbot. Blake was single, a homeowner with good credit. Bad credit could get him busted out of the military, which was true for every military officer because it made him or her vulnerable to corruption and being recruited by foreign entities for nefarious purposes. In short, Grant grunted, they had nothing on Blake…except for Gracie's identifying him as the man who'd given her the black rose at the Christmas program and as the man mowing a lawn he shouldn't have been mowing near Della's cottage when her garage exploded.

While Grant didn't dismiss Gracie's certainty that Blake had been that man, he didn't want to rely solely on a kid's memory for evidence of it. "We need more," he told Madison.

She nodded, walked into the kitchen and called back, "I didn't find anything even suggesting he's crazy enough to do the things Blue Shoes did." She walked back into the dining room with a plate of cheese and crackers. "The worst thing about him is he's incredibly ambitious." She bit a cracker and slowly chewed, then set the plate down on the table between her and Grant. "Whether Blake is ambitious enough to get caught in the middle is the question."

Grant reached for a cracker and sliced a piece of Gouda from the disc. "Between Dayton and Talbot?"

Madison took her seat. "Yes—not necessarily in realizing all that was going on, but he could have been covering his bases on whether or not Talbot and Dayton got their promotions."

"I'm not sure I'm tracking." Grant popped the cracker into his mouth. The crunching sound of his biting down followed.

Madison leaned back. "I think Blake is ambitious enough to make sure he's in line for his next promotion whichever way Talbot's and Dayton's promotions went. If Talbot snagged the congressional appointment and Dayton took over the Nest, Blake wanted to be on his good side and positioned to move up. If Talbot wasn't promoted and kept the Nest command, then Blake wanted to be on his good side and positioned to move up the chain with him." Madison leaned forward. "From the calls coming in and the correspondence going out, Blake had to know that Talbot was keeping Dayton in the dark about things."

"No way around that, unless Talbot handled all his own correspondence and calls."

"How likely is that?" Madison asked.

"Not impossible but highly improbable." Grant took a drink of his iced tea. "Especially when he's commanding the facility everyone knows about and one few know about. That's double duty."

Madison stared at the boards on the walls, at the green Blake timeline. "It might be helpful to call a few of his prior commanders and get their impressions."

"They'll want to know the reason."

Madison looked from the photo of Blake back to Grant. "Tell them the reason is classified."

"They're generals, Madison."

"Yes, they are." She smiled. "Who knows better that classified means classified and, when the military's involved, violations create security breaches that endanger lives?"

"Good point." Grant wiggled his fingers. "Pass me that file."

Madison handed it to him, but didn't let go. "We make a good team, don't we?"

"Yes, we do."

"Are you liking me any better than when we first left the Nest?"

"What do you mean?"

She hadn't brought this up because frankly she feared his response. But her feelings for him were deepening by the day—at times, by the hour—and in their beach run today, she'd reached the tipping point. For days now, they'd prayed and worked together, ate and went to church together. They exercised and grocery shopped and did everything else together she could dredge up in her mind that couples not yet committed do. And she'd loved it all. He seemed to love it all, but she wasn't falling for the appearance trap twice. He'd proven he was a master at it.

So she'd let things go unspoken and kept her questions to herself, but now, standing on the other side of the tipping point, she wanted answers. She had feared the developing bonds between them and the deeper feelings were one-sided and hadn't wanted to know the truth. Now she feared not knowing was worse. He could break her heart either way, but if that's the path they were on, better to break it now while she was neck-deep in this investigation than after it when her life returned to normal without him. She'd have way too much time on her hands then to mourn losing him.

"You were kind of eager to get away from me then," she reminded him.

"I tried to explain myself but you wouldn't listen."

True. "Do you know why?"

"Not really." He looked worried. "I talked to Mrs. Renault about it, not that it helped."

She hadn't mentioned it. "What did she tell you?"

"To give you some time to come to grips with everything."

"With you infiltrating my agency and my life. That's what you mean?"

He looked away. "Yes."

"You're worried about us." Madison saw and sensed it clearly.

"Aren't you?"

She pulled his pink stone out of her pocket. "Here." She passed it to him. "At the moment, you need this more than I do."

He took it. "So you're not going to trust me, after all."

"No, I absolutely do trust you."

Grant frowned, lifted the stone. "So why are you giving this back?"

"Because you just look worried."

"Madison, if I know nothing else, I know that with you there is no 'just' in anything. You're deliberate. So spare me the mental gymnastics and tell me what this really means."

"It means, rub it. It clears your thinking and you need a clear mind when talking to Blake's former generals." She folded her hands in her lap. "And about us," she said, putting a bite in her tone. "We're fine. Better than fine. I'm thinking you're serious about me and I'm good with that. So if you're not, now's the time to say so. Am I just an assignment to you?" Laced in her lap, her hands shook. Her palms went clammy.

He sobered, and looked her right in the eye. "You've never been just an assignment to me."

Joy burst inside her. She bit the smile from her lips. "Really?" Did she dare to believe him? To trust him with knowing he had her heart?

He sighed. "I'm crazy about you, Madison, and I don't want to go anywhere. I'd rather be here with you, working on a case that makes me sick inside, than anywhere else."

She did smile then, and reached for his hand. "Me, too."

"No more worrying for either of us. We're fine."

She'd told him that earlier. "Yes, we're fine." And they were, at least for now. Considering she hadn't let a man this far into her inner circle since Afghanistan, she was content with that. "It's Friday and the generals could be skating out early. Better make those calls."

"Right." Grant pecked a kiss to her palm, then released her hand and picked up the phone.

Just before six, Grant joined her in the kitchen at the granite breakfast bar. "Well?" She dished up Chinese food from the cartons into bowls. "Hope this is okay?"

"Smells great and I'm starving."

She smiled and passed him a spoon. "Grab a plate."

He reached, and said, "I talked to his last two bosses. Our take on Blake's ambition is confirmed. Both of them said he had a reputation for making sure that however a situation resolved, he had skin in the game on the right side."

"So he habitually plays both sides."

Grant nodded, and dropped the spoon into a bowl of lemon chicken. "They're emailing reports over, recapping what they said."

"That's good." Left nothing to get muddled up in translation when it was all down in black and white. It was raining again, so Madison took a seat at the kitchen table.

Grant joined her, his plate heaping.

That pleased her. She hadn't asked what he wanted. They'd had Chinese multiple times in the past months and she knew his preferences. That surprised her. She hadn't realized how many things about him she'd absorbed.

"Any important news from the office?" he asked.

"Mrs. Renault says everything's under control." They'd been so focused on what they were doing here that Madison had left the agency completely under Mrs. Renault's watchful eye. "I have to admit, a part of me resents that they don't need me more."

Grant bit into an egg roll. "They rely on you for everything. Think about it, Madison. Even if things were falling apart, Mrs. Renault would deal with them because she has a pretty good idea what you're dealing with here."

"Talbot's probably told her exactly what we're doing. I'm not sure." She frowned. "You know how close-mouthed Mrs. Renault is unless she knows exactly what she's talking about."

"I've noticed that about her."

Madison frowned. "Shifting focus. So they wouldn't worry about their reports and what us asking for them really meant."

Grant nodded. "Not that Mrs. Renault would lie."

"No, but she's a master at saying just enough to lead you to believe what she wants you to believe. You have to do the jumping to conclusions, though."

"After dinner, let's look at what Blake might have found on Dayton that cued him Dayton could be Blue Shoes."

"If Blake did find something, how he used it could be significant to us." A memory at the Nest flashed through her mind. Her in the duct, staring down into Janet Hardy's cell. "He didn't treat Janet well, when she was detained."

"Talbot claims he knew nothing about her detention."

"I believe him about that," Madison said. "When I told him she was there, he was shocked." Madison swept her hair back. "Blake did exactly what Dayton told him in there. I witnessed that myself." Another memory flashed through her mind. "Grant, when you were in my cell pretending to be me, and Dayton was on his way down there, Blake tried to call him, right?"

Grant nodded.

"On his mobile?"

"No, at the operations desk. I didn't see it, but I heard

Beecher take the call and tell Dayton who it was. Dayton blew Blake off."

Madison felt the hair on her neck lift. "He didn't take the call?"

"No."

What did that mean? She mulled it over.

Grant paused, his fork midair. "Blake had to be on the inside with Dayton or he wouldn't have given Gracie the flower and he wouldn't have been on scene with a lawn mower to watch Della's garage blow." Pausing, Grant sobered. "I know what Blake wanted and what Dayton promised him."

"What?"

"He was going to make Blake his vice."

Madison drew back. "He's a lieutenant."

"Yes. And he'd be promoted below the zone and probably be youngest vice commander ever. Certainly the youngest at the Nest."

Madison sucked in a breath. "Blake would sell his soul for that."

"I fear he did."

"I think it's time we talked to Blake." Madison worried her lower lip. Grant still held the pink rubbing stone in his hand and his thumb moved rapidly across the face of it.

She couldn't blame him. Especially when she had her left hand in her pocket, rubbing her own Purple Heart.

Madison and Grant spoke briefly with Beecher at the Nest cellblock's observation desk.

"Any trouble?" Grant asked.

"None," Beecher said. "I'm not sure they're even aware they're in the same cellblock. I haven't seen any signs of it. I moved Dayton up to the first cell—I trust him the least, and it's closest to the desk. Blake's at the far end."

"You can be sure Dayton's noticed people delivering food to Blake, if nothing else." Madison crossed her chest with her arms.

"If he turned around once in a while, he might. But he just sits on the floor all day and night with his back to the bars."

Grant rubbed his jaw. Dayton was accustomed to being free to do pretty much what he wanted. He'd resent having his every move watched. "When I was in Madison's cell and Dayton came down here," Grant said, "you remember him getting a call at the desk?"

Beecher nodded. "Blake had something he wanted to tell Dayton, but he never got the chance. Dayton didn't take the call."

That's what Grant wanted verified. "Would you write that out for me?"

"For your report?"

Apparently Talbot had filled Beecher in. Grant nodded.

"We're going to talk to Blake," Madison said before Beecher could ask questions she didn't want to answer.

"I'll have a statement waiting for you when you come back."

They walked down the cellblock's center corridor.

Being here again had Madison edgy. Every nerve ending in her body sizzled its rebellion.

"You okay?"

"I'm telling myself I am." She glanced over. "But I'll be glad when we're out of here."

"Understood."

As they walked past, Dayton didn't look over.

They stopped outside Blake's cell.

He rushed the bars. "It's about time."

"For what?" Grant asked.

"For someone to remember I'm stuck here." He gestured wildly. "I've been locked up for over a week and you guys and Beecher are the only people I've seen. What kind of treatment is this?"

"The kind you should expect when you do the things you've done."

"What have I done? Nothing to deserve this, that's for sure." His eyes stretched wide.

"Dayton claims you're Blue Shoes," Madison said.

"What?" Blake was just outraged enough to be credible.

Neither Madison nor Grant answered.

"I'm not Blue Shoes." Blake paced his cell, his movements highly agitated. "I can't believe the commander would believe that for a second."

"We didn't say he did," Grant told Blake. "I think we should pull up a couple chairs and you tell us exactly what's been going on here."

"Fine by me." Blake grabbed his cot and heaved, dragging it close to the bars, then plopped down on it.

Grant grabbed two folding chairs from a stack at the end of the corridor, then set them up outside Blake's cell.

Madison pulled out a recorder. "Ready?"

Blake nodded.

She turned the recorder on, stated the date, time and that the conversation was being recorded with permission, which Blake verified, then they began.

Grant posed the first round of questions.

It netted them nothing. Madison tried the second and it proved fruitless, too.

Two full hours later, Grant said, "You're wasting our time."

"I'm telling you what I know."

"You're telling us what you think we want to hear," Grant said. "Look, I'm not going to sugarcoat this. You've got a reputation for covering bases so you're protected regardless of the outcome. That's worked well for you in the past, but you're in a lot of trouble here, and your tactics aren't going to work well for you this time. You've got one shot to ever walk out of here, and this is it. Without us, you're not going to make it."

His arms propped on his knees, Blake let his head hang for a long minute. When he looked up, his misery reflected in his eyes. "Dayton promised me the vice slot here," he said, then swallowed hard. "I didn't know he was Blue Shoes. I swear it."

Madison kept her reaction to herself, but asked, "Why were you outside Della's cottage when the garage exploded?"

"What's that got to do with this?"

"Just answer the question," she said. "You were seen mowing the lawn across the street, but disappeared after the explosion."

"I was told to watch her. At the time, she was suspected of a security breach."

"You had nothing to do with the explosion, then? Is that what you're saying?"

"Of course I didn't." He frowned. "I was there, but I wasn't mowing the lawn."

"A witness places you at the mower."

"I was at it. It was running, and I was watching it while Dayton got a bottle of water. He left the mower running, and I thought someone ought to watch it. There are kids in that neighborhood, you know? One was sitting out on the porch across the street."

Gracie. "So where did Dayton go to get the bottle of water?"

"His truck, I guess. I honestly didn't notice. He left, the garage blew and it got chaotic fast."

Grant and Madison exchanged a look. That's all they'd be getting from Blake on that.

Shifting on his seat, Grant took over. "Let's move forward to Christmas Eve and the children's program at church."

"I was there."

"We know," Grant said. "You gave a little girl a black rose."

He looked puzzled, then his expression cleared. "Yeah, I did. I'd forgotten." He rubbed at his forehead.

"I don't remember her name, but I did give her a rose. She was dressed up for the play."

"If you don't know her, why did you give her the flower?"

"It wasn't actually for her. It was for Maggie Mason. I passed along a message, too. That her red dress was pretty or something like that. I don't recall the exact words now. It was pretty insignificant."

"Try to recall the exact message," Madison advised him.

"Why? It was a kids' play and a flower for a woman wearing a pretty dress. It was nothing."

"It was a very big something, Blake," Grant said. "You realize two bombs were in the church that night, and more in the parking lot."

He frowned. "I knew a car bomb went off in the parking lot, but I didn't know there were bombs in the church."

Madison grunted. "Have you been under a rock? It was all over the news and, by your own admission, you were there."

"I delivered the rose, and then left and went straight to the flight line."

"Why?" Grant asked.

"Because I had orders to go to Iraq for three weeks." Irritation bled through in his tone. "Where are you going with this stuff? Neither of these things has anything to do with what happened here."

"Actually, both do," Madison said. "The rose you delivered..." He nodded, and she went on. "It was the signature of a serial killer after Maggie Mason, the woman in the pretty red dress. Gary Crawford's signature."

The color leaked out of Blake's face. "No."

"Yes." Madison leaned forward. "I have a question, and, Blake, you'd better tell me the truth or we're done here."

The gravity of his situation was coming into focus; it showed in every drawn line on his face. "I will."

"You said you were delivering the rose with a message about the dress for Maggie through this child."

He nodded.

"For whom?"

Anguish crossed his face. "I can't say."

Grant sighed. "A flower and pretty dress hardly rise to the level of being classified."

"I don't make the rules, I just follow them," Blake fired back.

"One more question," Madison interrupted. "Did you sign or deliver a written order to Janet Hardy that directed her to expunge telephone records?"

"I'm not authorized to sign those orders, and I didn't sign them. But I did deliver several of them to her."

That surprised Madison. She'd been playing a hunch in asking, and now she was glad she had.

"Who signed them?"

"Some were generated by the commander and some by Dayton. I don't know which one you mean. Can you be more specific?"

Grant nodded. "Of greatest interest is the one directing Janet Hardy to expunge the records of a call to WKME's station manager, Brett Lund."

His face went ruddy. "I remember it, but I don't honestly remember who signed it. I'd tell you if I knew, but I'd be guessing."

The sorry thing about that answer was Madison totally believed him. She stood up. "That's all for now."

"Are you going to get me out of here?"

"We're going to complete our investigation," Grant said.

The man's fate was in higher hands, and all three of them knew it.

Madison left the cellblock and then the building and was glad to be outside. "What do you think?" she asked Grant.

"I think he was played and set up. I don't think he's Blue Shoes." He crossed the parking lot. "Do you?"

"No, but I do believe he's hiding something. I'm not sure what or for whom."

Grant frowned, but kept his thoughts to himself. "Let's go talk to Janet Hardy."

"It's after eleven, Grant," Madison reminded him. "We'll talk to her first thing in the morning." When they were seated in his Jeep, Madison added, "I'm assuming you want to know why Janet didn't say Blake delivered the expunge orders and claimed not to know who signed them."

"You'd be correct."

"I'm eager to hear her answers to those things myself."

TEN

When Grant and Madison arrived on the West Side cul-de-sac, Janet Hardy was in her front yard on her knees, weeding her flowerbeds.

Serene, hands in the dirt and humming, she looked over and saw them walking toward her. Her smile faded.

Madison nodded. "Good morning, Janet."

"It was." Janet stood up and removed her gardening gloves. "What is it now?"

Definitely still wary, but after being locked up for as long as she had been, Madison could certainly understand why. "Just a few questions."

"Dayton and Blake?"

"Still behind bars."

Her sigh of relief lifted her shoulders. "That means you're here for…"

Madison looked her right in the eye. "The truth."

She smiled. "I'm ready to give it to you, now that I'm not locked up like a rat in a trap anymore."

"You have the order to expunge the phone record?" A chill went up Madison's spine.

"Not exactly." She crooked a finger at them to come with her inside. When the door shut behind them, she walked on. "My computer's in here."

They followed her down a narrow hallway to an extra bedroom, where she had her computer sitting on a whitewashed desk. Craft items were stacked in plastic boxes against the wall. "I couldn't tell you Blake brought me the order—not with him watching my every move," she explained.

Understanding now, Madison said, "That was your only leverage to ever get out."

Janet Hardy nodded, her hair swinging toward her face. "If they found that order, I was as good as dead, and I knew it."

"You said you don't have the order," Grant reminded her.

"I don't. It was misfiled, and they haven't found it yet, though I expect they've been looking high and low for it."

Madison got a glimpse of how the woman's mind worked. "They're not going to find it, are they?"

"Doubtful." She smiled. "Let's say I have a unique filing system for questionable documents."

"You can get it."

"Actually, I can't." She booted up her computer. "But I don't need it." She tapped an electronic device next to her computer. "I have this."

"An external hard drive?"

"A scanner." She dipped her chin. "Anything comes across my desk that makes me the least bit uneasy, I scan myself a copy and store it in a secret location." She sniffed. "It's sad we live in a world where people tell you to do things, then get convenient amnesia. It happens a lot, I'm sorry to say, so I keep myself a CYB book."

"CYB?" Grant asked, clearly puzzled.

"Cover your back." Janet lifted her chin. "I'll take my hits for my mistakes, but nobody's gonna lie about me and get away with it."

Madison had called her backup by a different name but she knew exactly what Janet meant. "You've got a scan of the original order." Madison swallowed a gasp.

She twirled her finger. "I need to log in."

They turned their backs and waited for Janet's signal.

"Okay." She hit Print, and pointed to the screen. "There it is."

Grant reached for the printed copy. "You have any problem in attesting to this being a certified copy of the original?"

"No problem whatsoever."

Madison scanned the screen but couldn't see who'd signed it. She looked at Grant, reading the printed copy. His expression gave nothing away. "Well?" she asked.

"Dayton."

Madison looked at Janet. "What about this order made you flag it? Why did it make you uneasy?"

"Because Talbot always signed them himself. I thought it was weird for Dayton to sign one without the commander's initialing it, as well."

"Just how many of these are there?" Grant asked.

"Over the last four years, probably three or four dozen."

"Can you give us copies of them, too?"

"I can, but I don't know if I should. The commander—"

"We have his full authority," Grant told Janet. "Access to whatever we need."

Madison couldn't speak. She tried, but her voice just wasn't there. She was too stunned.

"You okay?" Grant whispered while Janet printed out the documents.

"When Maggie was running from Crawford, his calls were routed through the base and rerouted to various military installations around the world." Madison looked at Grant. "Why would the commander expunge those records? They were evidence used to convict Crawford."

"I don't know." He frowned. "But I think we'd better hold this information in reserve until we do."

He wanted to exclude it from the preliminary report. A sickening feeling sank in the pit of her stomach and she nodded her agreement.

When they left Janet Hardy's house, the first words out of Grant's mouth were the very ones going through Madison's mind.

"We need to run a timeline on Talbot."

They did. She pulled out the tape of their interview with Blake—replayed his answers about the rose. "Grant," she said, "Blake was holding back."

"What?"

"He never told us who asked him to deliver the rose. Just claimed it was classified. If it was Dayton, with him accusing Blake of being Blue Shoes, I'd think he'd have told us."

"Talbot." Grant slammed on the brakes and headed back to the Nest.

Their minds obviously were moving in the same dark direction, and it appeared Grant wanted to confirm or dispel those suspicions now.

"It can't be Talbot, Grant. It just can't." Madison felt chilled, betrayed to the bone. "Mrs. Renault will be devastated. I—I—"

"I don't want to believe it, either." Grant gripped the steering wheel hard. His knuckles were raised like knobs. "But remember what Mrs. Renault herself said."

"What?"

"Throw out preconceived notions and find the truth and—"

"Let the chips fall where they may." Madison feared those words would be burned into her memory forever. She closed her eyes and prayed they were wrong. Prayed with all her might that Talbot was the man Mrs. Renault believed him to be.

Two hours later, the proof was before Madison's eyes. Blake had confirmed that Talbot had asked him to deliver the rose to Gracie for Maggie with the message about her dress, and Talbot's timeline had more holes in it during peak crime times than a chunk of Swiss cheese.

Madison's disappointment was so profound, her eyes leaked tears.

Grant's, too, shone overly bright.

They hugged to comfort each other for a long moment, then Grant cleared his throat. "I need to make a call."

"Mrs. Renault?"

"Beecher," Grant said, dialing. When he answered, Grant told him he needed to speak directly to Blake.

A long few minutes later, Blake's familiar voice came through the phone. "Hello."

"Talbot's timeline has a lot of holes in it during peak times when Blue Shoes was active."

"Are you asking me a question, Deaver?"

"Drop the act. Trust me, you can't afford it. Where are the records?"

"Dayton's."

"So he pulled them?" Blake getting leverage on Dayton, Dayton getting leverage on Talbot. Wasn't anybody straight with anybody anymore?

"No, I pulled them," Blake admitted. "Insurance. Dayton likes to trash houses, and I figured when he couldn't find the logbook, he'd trash mine, looking for it. So I hid it at his house. I figured that's the one place he'd never trash."

"Where?"

"Spare bedroom, back of the closet, top shelf."

"You lied to me," Grant said, anger simmering in his voice. "You knew about Blue Shoes."

"Everyone knew about Blue Shoes. I just didn't know I knew him."

Grant stiffened. "Is he Talbot or Dayton?"

"My money's on Dayton, but I don't know for sure. If I did, I wouldn't be stuck in here, would I?"

He wouldn't. He'd be free or dead.

"Anything else we need to know?"

"I'm afraid not. It wasn't for a lack of trying, I can tell you that. I just couldn't decipher which of them was guilty."

Grant wished he didn't understand that dilemma.

Saturday afternoon Talbot phoned Grant, and asked for a preliminary report. Grant told the commander there were still too many unconfirmed loose ends but he and Madison would have one ready for him in a few days and that they were on the way in to interview Dayton.

"Anything unexpected come up so far?" Talbot asked.

Far too much on far too many. "A few surprises, but nothing conclusive yet, sir."

"Very well. Keep me posted."

"Yes, sir."

Madison clasped Grant's hand. "Does he know you're stalling him?"

"I don't think so. Not yet, anyway."

"Good." She didn't look forward to sleeping with one eye open until this was resolved.

Ten minutes later they sat outside Dayton's cell.

Madison recorded a lengthy diatribe of Dayton vowing that Talbot was Blue Shoes, and he hadn't done a thing he shouldn't have done.

Losing patience with the man, she asked, "What about hiring the skateboarder to plant the plastic mailbox in Della Jackson's purse?"

"Talbot asked me to as a favor. It was a private joke, he said." Dayton shrugged. "Poor taste, no matter how you slice it, but when a superior officer issues a direct order, you obey it. You both know that as well as I do."

Madison almost believed him. He hadn't said a word since his arrest, but seemed to have no problems now speaking his mind. The words flowed, and made solid sense. Dayton hadn't been idle while sitting on that cell floor with his back to the bars. He'd been planning and preparing for this moment and it had paid off. He presented himself well, articulate and convincing.

But, Madison wondered, was he being honest?

When after the interview she and Grant left the Nest, she still wasn't sure. "We need access to his house to pull the records Blake stashed there."

"We can't get it without Talbot's authorization."

"He gave us blank permission to do what needed doing." The glare hurt her eyes. Madison got out her sunglasses.

"Professionally, not personally. His office, no problem. But his home…"

State laws came into play. "Point taken." Madison thought it over. "Talbot expects us to do this. Call and ask him for express permission. If he denies it, then at least we made the attempt and that'll be included in the report."

Grant did and within a few minutes, they had Talbot's permission and Dayton's apartment address. A spare key was hidden in a rock near the back door.

Twenty minutes later, Madison and Grant walked through the apartment to make sure it was clear. Then they slowed down to look around.

Modern and minimalist, every room was chrome and clean-lined, and all the fabrics were white, navy and burgundy, including the dish towels folded neatly in the third drawer beside the stove.

"This is unnatural," she told Grant, who sat at the table, thumbing through the file Blake had hidden in the spare bedroom closet on the top shelf. Whether or not Blake actually had put the file there, it had been located exactly where he'd told them it would be. "No one lives like this."

Grant looked over at her. "Like what?"

"Look at this place." She lifted a hand. "Nothing is out of place. There isn't a speck of dust anywhere or even a piece of lint on the carpet. It's not natural."

"He lives alone, and he's been military all his adult life. You went through the training. You know even clothes folded in drawers are precisely placed."

She walked out of the kitchen. "I also know that as soon as that training is over, a normal person starts relaxing a little." She stepped back and opened a lower cabinet, then examined the bottoms of his pots. Not a mark on them. "These pots have never been used."

"Maybe he just bought them, or he hates to cook."

"Maybe." It didn't sit right with her. They'd started stacking evidence near the front door. "I'm going to check his computer."

Grant nodded. "This is definitely Talbot's logbook. We need to get back to your house, and add these entries to the timeline. See what it tells us about Talbot."

It could either clear him of wrongdoing, or further implicate him. "I won't be long."

In the spare bedroom she sat down at the computer and went to work. Half an hour later, her frustration was building. His desktop computer had no saved files. Not one. Finding that too peculiar, she checked recent files and history—and found a plethora of evidence. "Grant," she called out, her heart thumping hard.

He came in. "What?"

"It's all here." She pointed to the screen. "Maps and driving directions, flights, research on making bombs… He even ran Gary Crawford and did an exhaustive study on him and all the public information on his murders." Madison scanned the file list. "Brett Lund, David Pace and Beth Crane are on here, too."

"Let's disconnect it and take it with us."

Madison and Grant worked all night and at ten the next morning read the final draft of their report. The logbook cleared Talbot, and the computer data squarely pointed to Dayton. Everything now pointed to Dayton, except the rose to Maggie, and Blake could be deliberately misleading them on that.

Grant poured Madison yet another cup of coffee. "You satisfied with our determinations and findings?"

"We've turned every stone we can find and presented the facts based on the evidence. That's all we can do."

"Let's take it to Talbot, then."

Madison drove them out to the facility. Grant phoned on the way to let the commander know they were coming, and when they arrived, Beecher sent them right into Talbot's office.

Grant passed their report. "Here you go, sir."

"Thank you." He took it. "Would you two mind hanging around while I review it, in case there are any questions?"

"No, sir. We'll step out." Grant opened the office door and he and Madison stepped through to Beecher's office.

He closed a file stamped "confidential" and rested his arm atop it. "You two look beat."

"It's been a long couple weeks," Madison said.

Grant nodded. "Especially the last twenty-four hours."

"Dayton's been expecting you to ask for the keys to his house."

"You mean his apartment," Grant said.

Beecher's expression turned to stone. "Dayton doesn't have an apartment."

Grant's and Madison's gazes collided. "Where's his home?" A sick feeling pitted Grant's stomach. Soured it.

"On the bay. Same neighborhood as Madison's."

"I've never seen him in my neighborhood," Madison whispered to Grant.

"Everything's in some kind of trust," Beecher said with a shrug. "He's loaded and single."

"How do you know this?" Grant asked.

"Just things I've heard around. You know how people talk." Madison's message bore down on Grant. Though unspoken, the context was clear. *We've been had.*

"Grant, Madison." Talbot appeared at his office door. "Well done." He smiled. "Leadership should have all it needs to make the call and determine their fates."

Talbot. He'd framed Dayton and Blake, and he'd used them to put the final nails in their coffins.

"Terrific," Grant said, not missing a beat. "We're done." He smiled at Madison. "I'm going to take you home, and we're both going to get some rest."

"Well deserved." He clapped them on the shoulders. "I'll send this in, and we'll close this unfortunate chapter of history at the Nest." He gave them a genuine look of gratitude. "I appreciate all you've done."

"You're welcome, sir." Grant nodded, slid Beecher a telling look, and then he and Madison left headquarters.

Neither of them said a word until they were in Madison's Jag and had passed the gate guards and left the installation.

Grant spoke first. "How do we handle this?"

Madison turned and headed toward her office. "We go to the one person we know we can trust, who will know exactly what to do and how to best do it."

"Mrs. Renault?"

"Exactly."

* * *

In the Lost, Inc., conference room forty minutes later, Mrs. Renault had been briefed—and had aged ten years. She showed them the interior of a continuity log that was purportedly Talbot's. "The one Blake planted at the apartment wasn't the real one. This one is." Mrs. Renault thumbed the pages.

"It's blank."

"Yes, it is. And when tests are done on the fake one, and they date the entries, it'll be proven fraudulent. Andrew didn't record entries because he didn't want any records of his activities."

"Why would he do this?"

"I have my suspicions and they include counterintelligence. That's all I'm free to say." She stood and stepped away from the conference-room table, dialed a number from memory and then waited.

"Chairman Sayers, please. Renée Renault."

Grant whispered to Madison, "She's calling the Chairman of the Joint Chiefs of Staff?"

"Apparently."

Minutes later, Mrs. Renault launched into a succinct, detailed briefing. "What shall we do?"

A moment later she hung up the phone. "We're to stay put together until Beecher notifies us Andrew is in custody."

"Beecher?" Grant frowned. "How do we know for sure whose side he's on?"

"He's one of mine." Mrs. Renault smiled. "Where do you think I got Talbot's real log?"

Madison's heart felt squeezed. "I'm so sorry, Mrs. Renault." She had to be hurt deeply by Talbot's betrayal.

"So am I." Sadness permeated her eyes. "I respected him once."

"How long will it be before he's taken into custody?"

"Minutes." She hiked her chin. "Beecher filed a preliminary report with me earlier today, so we were prepared. Just waiting for your full report."

"You keep saying *we,*" Madison noted. "I get the feeling that you're not just the former spouse of—"

She gave Madison an enigmatic smile. "I'm exactly who you believe me to be, Madison. I just come with… shall we say, perks."

Former Intel. She had to be former Intel. That's the only way her insider connections made sense. "What were you doing professionally when you and John met?"

She smiled again, and didn't say a word.

The phone rang. She stared at it. "That'll be Beecher, telling us it's done."

"Hello." Madison answered the phone.

"Madison, may I speak to Mrs. Renault, please."

Madison passed the phone. "Beecher."

Mrs. Renault listened. "Thank you. Me, too." She slowly put down the phone. "Andrew is in custody at the Nest. Two in the loop are inbound to sort everything out."

"Does Beecher need help?" Grant asked.

"No, he brought in his explosives team—they're all mine—so everything is under control."

"I believed it was Dayton."

"You suspected Talbot," Grant said.

"We both did. But I hoped it wouldn't be him."

Mrs. Renault swept a hand over Madison's shoulder. "You two have been through a lot, and not only have you handled it well, you've given the loop what it needs to protect us all." She squeezed Madison's shoulder. "I'm proud of you."

Madison wasn't a fool. They hadn't surprised Mrs. Renault with any of this. "How long have you known Talbot was Blue Shoes?"

"Not long." She hiked her chin. "Grant, will you be staying with us at Lost, Inc., or returning to active duty?"

"It depends." He looked at Madison.

"Ah, of course." She sent him an encouraging look.

"What about Dayton and Blake?" Madison asked.

"Your report combined with what we have—they'll be held accountable for their infractions, no more and no less."

The disclosure was less than Madison hoped for and more than she expected. "And the Nest?"

"Will stay prepared."

That's what it was. Madison recalled the exercise with the trucks and boxes. They weren't coded. Seeds were seeds, water was water and purifier was a water purification tablet. It was a doomsday preparatory facility, to assure that resources were available if and when needed. And a place to detain those with access to high-level, classified information that carried high risks if placed elsewhere.

"I'm still not clear on why Talbot asked us to investigate," Madison said. "He couldn't call in the inspector general because it would broaden the need-to-know loop. But why us?"

Mrs. Renault dipped her chin, and gave Madison the infamous brow lift. "He thought after helping you, you'd dismiss evidence against him."

Grant nodded. "Loyalty. He knew how much it meant to you, Madison, and how much getting you out of detention meant to me."

Mrs. Renault smiled. "It was a reasonable expectation. You are both loyal. He just misjudged to what." Madison must have seemed puzzled, because Mrs. Renault added, "Your loyalty is to God, truth and your nation. That's far bigger than any one man."

Madison wrapped her mind around it all.

"I'm taking the rest of the day off," Mrs. Renault told Madison. "If you want me, call my mobile. I'll be at the Emerald Grand in Destin."

"Why? You're welcome to use my beach house."

"Thank you, but no. I need some time to myself." She frowned. "Andrew trashed my home and destroyed everything I had of John's. I need time alone with my memories." At the door, she paused and looked back at them. "Love is far too rare to squander because we allow ourselves to forget."

Profound words. Ones Madison took into her heart.

Mrs. Renault left, and Grant stepped to Madison's side. "I think her heart is broken."

"She'll miss John's things. They've kept him close to her."

"I think she was beginning to fall in love with Talbot," Grant said.

"I hope not." Madison looked at Grant. "She trusted him, and he betrayed her. That, and destroying what she had left of John, well, it's a lot to make a woman bitter."

"I betrayed you," Grant whispered, his Adam's apple bobbing. "Are you bitter?" The look in his eyes spoke directly to her heart.

"Your situation was very different. You were caught between the proverbial rock and hard place—torn loyalties between your duty to your country and your heart." Empathy filled her. "I expect you spent a lot of time on your knees about it all."

"I did." He frowned. "Trying to keep right with God and do what I had to do…it wasn't easy."

"It rarely is."

"So why wouldn't you let me explain myself?"

She'd been waiting for this. "I've prayed a lot, too. We've been together for four months—"

"Almost five."

"Almost five." She smiled. "But all of it was time under challenges. Suspicions and doubts and—"

"One crisis after another."

"Exactly." She paused, framed her thoughts. "I know we care about each other, but we've never been together when we weren't in crisis with each other. I wasn't sure I could trust my feelings or that you should trust yours."

"Until we got you out of the Nest, that was true,"

he said. "But we've been pretty normal since then—you and me, I mean. We've still been dealing with unusual things."

"Unusual is normal at Lost, Inc." She shrugged. "Comes with the territory."

He searched her face. "So what are you saying?"

"I told you before. I was worried that in normal times you'd no longer be interested."

"That's what the waiting to talk has really been about. A delay tactic."

She nodded. "It was important to know if when we're normal the spark would still be there, or if you'd…" Her throat closed. She couldn't say it.

"Leave you?"

As she'd been left in Afghanistan. She nodded, and stepped out in faith. "I don't want to lose you."

"I don't want to lose you, either." He paused, waited for her to meet his gaze. "The spark will always be there. I love you, Madison."

Her heart stopped, then beat hard and fast, pumping wonder and contentment through her entire body. "Really?"

He smiled, stroked her face with such tenderness. "Really."

Shaky, breathless, she pulled the Purple Heart from her pocket and studied the scratch he'd made in it. A heart. He'd given it back to her when she'd been detained in the Nest, but she had been too afraid of being wrong to dream about what it meant. After her release, knowing he'd been ordered into her life, she didn't dare.

But the more they were together, working in tandem on different adversarial challenges, the more confident she grew; more daring and sure of him and of herself. *Her* daily devotionals became *their* daily devotionals. Not dreaming with the man who freely admitted you left him breathless, who chiseled at the shield around your heart until it crumbled—a shield you believed so thick and strong it would never fail—a man who opened his heart to his Lord with you as you opened yours seemed…cowardly. She lifted the medal. "I hoped that's what this heart meant."

"It didn't. Sorry." He cupped her face, his voice softened, thickened, burgeoning with intense emotion. "That heart meant 'forgive me,' for not being able to tell you the truth. Love came before then."

Her emotions rose and fell like a wild wave. Disappointment, then elation. "When you gave me the pink stone?"

"Earlier."

Madison took in a deep breath. He was a good man. Honorable, and he'd been there for her and with her every step of the way. She looked at the medal in her hand, dragged her fingertip over the scratched heart he'd etched into it, then lifted her gaze to his. "I gave this to you once after telling you what it symbolized to me. I'd like to give it to you again now, but the meaning of it has changed."

"Trust me, Madison."

She nodded and held out the medal. "I'm giving you this because I can't give you my heart." His face fell. She cupped his hands on her face. "That came out wrong."

"Thank God."

"I do. For everything, but most of all for you." She licked at her lower lip, her mouth dust-dry. "I can't give you something I don't have to give anymore."

"Are you still thinking you're incapable of loving anyone?"

"No." She pressed her thumbs to his lips. "You already have my heart. I love you, Grant."

Dawning washed over his face, and his joy was remarkable. It showed in every line, in the twinkle sparkling in his eyes. He tucked the medal in his pocket, then kissed the woman who so feared losing him, and with her heart wide open for the first time since being taken POW, Madison kissed him back.

With hard work and by the grace of God, she had healed.

Madison McKay was no longer lost.

She had made peace with her past, herself and with Grant, and safe in his arms, she knew never again would they be divided by torn loyalties.

* * * * *

Dear Reader,

Being caught between a rock and a hard place is never easy, and yet most of us at some time end up there. We walk in faith, try hard to keep our priorities straight and do the right thing for the right reason. But at times that doesn't protect us from challenges; it plants us in the middle of them. We do our best, but the thing that guides and sustains us, our faith, is the very thing that forces us to choose sides. And we choose knowing that we'll disappoint others, perhaps hurt those we most want not to hurt.

Such is the case for Grant Deaver and Madison McKay in *Torn Loyalties.* Madison gave her oath, and was abandoned. She endured and reclaimed her life, but wore the scars of betrayal and shielded herself from then on from further wounds. Then Grant Deaver comes into her life, and he chips at that shield. But Grant is a conflicted man, torn between duty and his heart. He can be loyal to one or the other, but not to both.

Madison and Grant discover that trust is a fragile thing. Once broken, it can seem impossible to repair. But if they have the courage to stay in faith, and forgive and trust anyway, they can discover a blessing that carries them through their darkest hour, and when it's done, discover their hearts have opened and healed.

That's Madison and Grant's story. It captured the

wonder of courage and leaps of faith in me, and I hope it will in you, too.

May you and your special someone have a Valentine's Day that captures your heart!

Blessings,
Vicki Hinze

Questions for Discussion

1. Madison McKay was abandoned and betrayed. It left scars that make it difficult for her to trust. Have you experienced a sense of betrayal? How did you cope with the aftermath of it?

2. Grant Deaver made an oath to serve and protect his country. But his duties put him between the proverbial rock and hard place. Where he can keep his oath, or betray a trust that is very important to him. He's a victim of torn loyalties and wants to do the right thing. Have you been in that position—caught between the rock and hard place? What did you do? How did it work out? If it happened again now, with the benefit of your experience, what, if anything, would you do differently?

3. Appearances can be deceptive. What we see often isn't the way things really are, or who someone really is inside. Have you ever thought something about another that seemed true but wasn't? Thought someone was one type of person but they turned out to be a very different type of person? How did your relationship with that person change?

4. Some manipulate or deceive us because they must. Others manipulate and deceive us deliberately.

Both manipulations and deceptions hurt. But which is easier to understand and forgive?

5. One of the lessons discovered in *Torn Loyalties* is that when trust is broken, it can seem impossible to repair, and yet a way does exist. Have you ever suffered a broken trust, then found a way to recover from it? Did that recovery result in trusting that person again?

6. Madison suffered betrayal and abandonment and the resulting pain had her shielding herself from further pain by sealing herself off emotionally and not letting others get close. She wholly trusted only one person. Having gone through betrayal and abandonment, can a person of faith forgive and forget unscarred? Or do the scars change that person in a way that enables them to take emotional risks in spite of them?

7. Grant walks an emotional tightrope, torn between duty and loyalty. His integrity and personal honor is on the line. He strives to stay right with God and do what he must do, which makes him appear to be someone he's not and forces him to do things he would prefer not to do. In that situation, how would you see yourself? How would you feel others perceive you? How do you cope with the challenges that creates?

8. At one point in the story, Grant fears losing a woman he cares for deeply and yet he is forced to do something he knows will hurt her. Have you experienced a situation where you had no choice but to hurt someone you loved? How did it impact your relationship? Did the relationship survive?

9. In a crisis, too often we seek God's help as a last resort. In *Torn Loyalties,* after betrayal, Madison and Grant pray together, attend church together and get to know each other in reverse, so to speak. The result is a deeper bond and new levels of trust. In discovering each other, in a sense, they discover themselves. Have you found that to be the case in your life?

10. During the darkest times, Madison and Grant can't see a way forward that ends with them being together. Both fear a future for them is impossible, but they continue to believe and hope anyway, and God steps in and makes a way. Have you been in a hopeless situation or relationship where there was no way for things to work out and yet they did? What wisdom did you gain from that experience?

11. On the whole issue of torn loyalties, what gems of wisdom have you gained that you can pass on to others?

SPECIAL EXCERPT FROM

Rookie K-9 officer Valerie Salgado saw a murder suspect leaving the scene of a crime and now needs protection.

Read on for a preview of the next book in the exciting TEXAS K-9 UNIT *series, GUARD DUTY by Sharon Dunn.*

"K-9 unit 349. Convenience-store robbery, corner of State and Grand. Suspects on the run."

Rookie officer Valerie Salgado hit her sirens and sped up. She reached the store, opened the back door of the patrol car and her Rottweiler, Lexi, jumped out.

Lexi found the trail, then ran hard, leading Valerie up the street, through an alley and into a residential neighborhood.

Lexi stopped suddenly in a yard that had stacks of roofing shingles piled on the walkway and a ladder propped against the roof.

The bushes in the yard shook. Valerie lifted her head just in time to see a man take off running.

Valerie clicked Lexi off the leash. Lexi leaped over the fence and bounded after the suspect.

Valerie unsnapped the holster that held her gun. She heard a scraping noise right before something crashed hard against her shoulder, knocking her to the ground.

She stumbled to her feet. Shingles. Was the second perpetrator on the roof? She hurried most of the way up the ladder using the roofline for cover.

The suspect came out from behind the chimney, aiming his gun at her. He slipped on the sharply angled

LISEXP0213

roof, falling on his side and dropping the gun. The gun skittered across the shingles and fell to the ground below. This was her chance.

Valerie scrambled up the ladder. "Put your hands up."

The man dashed toward her. He intended to push the ladder away from the roof!

The suspect's feet seemed to be pulled out from under him, and he slammed facedown on the roof. As the suspect scrambled to his feet, she saw the silhouette of a second man, tall and broad through the shoulders.

The second man landed a blow to the suspect's face, knocking him on his back.

Her rescuer stepped out of the shadows. "Officer Salgado, why don't you wait at the bottom? I'll stay up here and make sure this guy doesn't get any ideas."

She had no idea who this man was or where he had come from, but everything about him said law enforcement and he knew her name. "Who are you?"

Will Valerie's rescuer turn her life upside down?
Pick up GUARD DUTY by Sharon Dunn,
available March 2013 from Love Inspired Suspense.

To Trust or Not to Trust a Cowboy?

Former Dallas detective Jackson Stroud was set on moving to a new town for his dream job, until he makes a pit stop and discovers on the doorstep of a café an abandoned newborn and Shelby Grace, a waitress looking for a fresh start. He decides to help Shelby find the baby's mother, and through their quest he believes he's finally found a place to belong, while Shelby's convinced he will move on eventually. What will it take to convince Shelby that this is one cowboy she can count on?

Bundle of Joy

by

Annie Jones

Available March 2013!